KV-389-197

FORTUNE'S LADY

Upon the death of her godfather, beautiful Lady Rosalyn Tremayne inherits his large fortune, and in the spring of 1816 she returns to London after a prolonged absence. Her reappearance in the fashionable world causes much speculation. Has she decided that it is time to take a husband? Certainly there is no lack of admirers, including the fascinating yet wholly ineligible Rake Hellborn, whose expensive lifestyle demands an advantageous match.

Books by Melinda Hammond
in the Linford Romance Library:

SUMMER CHARADE

NEATH PORT TALBOT	
LIBRARIES	
CL	
DATE	
LOC.	
NO.	

TALBOT LIBRARIES
NEATH PORT

MELINDA HAMMOND

FORTUNE'S
LADY

Complete and Unabridged

LINFORD
Leicester

First published in Great Britain

First Linford Edition
published 1997

Copyright © 1982 by Melinda Hammond
All rights reserved

British Library CIP Data

Hammond, Melinda
    Fortune's lady.—Large print ed.—
    Linford romance library
    1. Love stories
    2. Large type books
    I. Title
    823.9'14 [F]

    ISBN 0–7089–5187–2

Published by
F. A. Thorpe (Publishing) Ltd.
Anstey, Leicestershire
Set by Words & Graphics Ltd.
Anstey, Leicestershire
Printed and bound in Great Britain by
T. J. International Ltd., Padstow, Cornwall

This book is printed on acid-free paper

1

THE house in Brook Street had been empty for the best part of the year, as indeed had been the case for the past decade, with the shutters closed and the knocker taken down, its owner, one Mr. Frencham, preferring the seclusion of his country estates to life in town. When it was known that this gentleman had died, however, there was much speculation as to what his heir would do with such a desirable residence.

It was not long before an army of workmen could be seen at the house, and this was taken as a sign that the new owner intended to occupy it.

"For, my dear Miss Trancher," as one elderly lady pointed out to her companion, "no-one would spend quite so much on refurbishing a house only to sell it."

It was with great interest therefore that these worthy ladies watched the arrival of an elegant travelling carriage one frosty morning the following spring. If the lady who descended from this vehicle noticed the twitch of the drapes from the neighbouring dwelling she gave no sign, merely looking up at the freshly painted properly with a slight smile, and giving any interested parties ample time to study her. She was a tall woman, who looked to be about five and twenty, although she was in fact some years older. She was dressed in a modish three-quarter pelisse of olive green, matched by a stylish bonnet of the same colour covering most of her luxuriant dark hair. She turned from her contemplation of the building as another woman descended from the carriage. She was seen to be considerably older than her companion, and neatly attired in dove grey, which proclaimed the widow.

"Well, Amelia, will you like my new home, do you think?"

"It is very grand, is it not?" replied the widow doubtfully.

The younger woman laughed and trod briskly up to the door.

"Come along, my dear, let us see how well my instructions have been carried out. Good morning, Potton, is everything in readiness for us?"

The butler, holding open the door for his mistress, bowed, assuring my lady that everything had been attended to, and uttering the hope that my lady had enjoyed a good trip.

"Tolerable, Potton, no more. The roads into London are not as good as I remember them, but perhaps my long absence had given my memory a rosier view." She turned once more to her companion, who had followed her into the hall. "This is Potton, my butler, Amelia. He was my cousin's first footman at Dowrings, and since he was about to wed the housekeeper on a neighbouring estate, it suited me very well to employ them both."

"And very grateful Mrs. Potton and

3

myself are to you, Lady Rosalyn," put in the young man earnestly, "we could not have managed so well without your help."

"Nonsense, Lord Dowring would have found a post for Mrs. Potton if I had not been in need of staff. As it is, things have worked out for the best. Now, I trust a room has been prepared for Mrs. Windhurst, as I ordered?"

"Yes, my lady." The butler turned with a slight bow to the widow. "If Madam would care to inspect the Pink Chamber?"

Mrs. Windhurst, escorted by a servant, set off up the wide staircase to her room, where her abigail, who had arrived some time before with the trunks and baggage, was busy unpacking. Meanwhile, Lady Rosalyn made a brief tour of inspection accompanied by her housekeeper, expressing her satisfaction at the way her orders had been carried out. Their tour ended in the large drawing-room, an elegant apartment at the front of the house. The room was freshly decorated, with new drapes at the window. The furniture was in the main that which Mr. Frencham had purchased many years ago, for, as Lady Rosalyn later informed Mrs. Windhurst, she found the style of Mr. Hepplewhite perfectly satisfactory, and saw no reason to replace it with the current fashion, which she did not like half so well.

"No indeed," agreed Mrs. Windhurst warmly, "I do not think that I should rest easily in my bed if I were surrounded by beasts' heads and feet, which seem so popular now — I am sure it would be no wonder if I were to wake up in the night screaming that I was being pursued by one of the chairs!"

Lady Rosalyn was much struck by this point of view, and said in a voice quivering with laughter, "That settles the matter, Amelia! I shall on no account allow such a thing to happen to you!"

The result of Lady Rosalyn's decision

was a charming mixture of old and new, creating an impression of quiet elegance to the house. Casting a look around the drawing-room, Lady Rosalyn turned to her housekeeper, anxiously awaiting her verdict. "I think we shall go on very nicely. I can see that you have already added a more homely touch to this room." She glanced at an arrangement of fresh flowers on one of the side tables.

Mrs. Potton flushed a little, pleased with this tribute.

"I hoped it might make you feel a little more at home, ma'am."

"And so it does. After living for so long in other people's homes, it is so comfortable to have a place of one's own!"

Lady Rosalyn repeated this sentiment to her cousin, when they retired to the drawing-room after dinner, and found that her feelings were shared.

"After dear Mr. Windhurst was taken, I lived for some time with my sister Lady Ashley, but I was so glad to get back to my own home, where I could order everything just as I liked!"

"Then I am sorry to have dragged you away, Amelia. I beg that you will tell me the moment you wish to return, for I would not keep you here unwillingly."

"Nonsense, Ros. You know I am only too happy to spend a few months with you in London. It is such an age since I was here that I shall positively enjoy escorting you to all the balls and parties, as well as shopping in all the most fashionable places! I am pleased you invited me."

"It was the least I could do after your kindness to me. If you had not come to my rescue I am sure I would have come to blows with my cousin!"

"It must have been very upsetting for you to see Harvey and Caroline in your old home," replied Mrs. Windhurst with ready sympathy.

"Oh no, dearest. I had already spent some months with my cousin after

Papa died, if you remember, when I passed over the reins of the estate, and helped them to settle in, although I did not think they were very grateful for my help. But that is understandable, for they had their own ideas of how they wished to go on at Dowrings. I think we were all very thankful when my Aunt Farradae offered to take me to Vienna, when my Uncle was posted there on some diplomatic mission. And then of course on to Brussels. When we had to return, I had nowhere else to go but to Harvey, although I made it clear that I would set about looking for an establishment of my own."

"But were you not alarmed with that Monster loose in Europe again, Ros? Your letters were always so full of gaiety and social calls that I thought you must be in a different world. The reports from Town were always so alarming."

"We were well behind the lines of battle, cousin, and with the Duke in command we knew that he would take great care to send us all home should we be in any danger, so we were able to carry on as if we were back in London."

"Well, whatever you say, I cannot but be glad that you are back with us now, and I swear, Rosalyn, that you do not look a day older than when you went away!" exclaimed Mrs. Windhurst, admiringly.

Indeed, Lady Rosalyn was becomingly attired that evening, having decided to honour the occasion by wearing a new gown of jonquil silk, a string of fine pearls clasped about her slender neck and a shawl of Norwich silk draped elegantly over her arms. At her cousin's comment, however, she laughed, but replied primly, "Why, Amelia, now that I am a wealthy woman, you have become a shocking toad-eater!"

"Rosalyn! I am nothing of the sort!" was the indignant reply, "and if you continue to laugh at me for speaking the truth I shall pack my bags and leave this instant!"

9

"Oh, Amelia, I beg you not to do that! Harvey would almost certainly insist that I take that tiresome relation of his as a companion if you leave me," exclaimed my lady in mock horror.

"Well I would not wish that old tabby on you," Mrs. Windhurst replied with unusual asperity. "I know Harvey is your cousin and I do not wish to cause you pain, my love, but Avis Mitchell has been his pensioner for years, and since she is suffering from one ailment or another whenever one meets her, one cannot suppose that she would make a satisfactory companion."

"It was only your promise to accompany me to Town that prevented him from foisting her on to me in the first place, and your assurance that you would escort me to all the most distinguished parties, which I have no wish to attend."

"What an absurd idea! A girl of your age will positively enjoy Ton parties."

Lady Rosalyn looked a little wistful.

"You forget, Amelia, I am eight and twenty."

"I do not, my love. You have convinced yourself that you are past praying for, when the truth is that you will beat most of the Town beauties to flinders! I have no doubt that it will not be long before you will be receiving any number of offers for your hand."

"I doubt I shall ever marry."

This was stated without emotion, and it slightly shocked Mrs. Windhurst, who said hastily, "Now, Rosalyn, I beg you will not say so. You do not know who you might meet, and it is not as if you are a nobody, after all. Besides, your journeys abroad brought you into contact with the most influential people."

"If they will accept me in Town. I am a jilt, you know," came the somewhat bitter reply.

"That was ten years ago, my love. The Ton has a short memory, and a fortune has always been a great help in overcoming prejudice," she added frankly.

Lady Rosalyn rose from her chair.

"It will make little difference, Amelia. I have my independence, which means a great deal to me, and I am looking forward to going to the theatres, visiting the sights and historical places far more than I am to attending the balls and parties you seem determined I should enjoy. It came to me while I was abroad that I know more about the capitals of Europe than I do of London; I intend to remedy that as soon as may be." She saw her cousin was looking dismayed, and stopped to plant a kiss on her brow.

"Please do not worry, Amelia, I shall not turn into an eccentric, I assure you. Tomorrow morning I will send off a few notes to those friends I know to be in Town, and I have no doubt I shall receive one from my sister in the next few days."

Lady Rosalyn was in part right. She did receive news of her sister, but not by letter. She was alone the following morning in the small salon at the back of the house, writing the letters she had promised to send, when Potton announced that her brother-in-law, Lord Carfax, was awaiting her in the drawing-room. Her pen spluttered on the page, and she was obliged to give her attention to blotting this before she could reply.

"Thank you, Potton. I shall be with him directly. Please arrange for refreshments to be taken to Lord Carfax."

She rose from the table and put a hand up to her hair, which was becomingly arranged in a knot high on her head, and dressed with a small spray of spring flowers. Small wisps of hair formed a charming frame for her face, which was now slightly flushed. With a perceptible straightening of her shoulders, my lady made her way to the drawing-room. As she entered, a gentleman standing by the window turned to face her. She saw before her a handsome gentleman, not much above thirty, with golden brown hair brushed into a semblance of disorder, and falling onto his wide brow.

His eyes were blue, set well apart beneath straight brows. His features were almost classical, and he was generally considered to be a very attractive gentleman. Lady Rosalyn did not disagree with this view, and she took in at a glance the impeccable morning-coat of blue superfine, and the tight-fitting pantaloons that showed his graceful figure to advantage. Although the light was behind him, she noted the crease in his brow, and the rather grim set of his mouth as he looked at her.

Lady Rosalyn held out her hand to her guest, and his brow cleared a little. He raised the hand to his lips before releasing it.

"I am glad to have found you at home, for I was not sure when you would arrive."

"We came to Town only yesterday, travelling direct from Mrs. Windhurst's home in Derbyshire."

His eyes never left her face, and she felt a little disconcerted. To cover her confusion she turned towards a sofa at one side of the fireplace.

"Pray be seated, sir. Amelia will be sorry to have missed you. She has gone shopping this morning."

"My errand is with you in any case, ma'am. When Cynthia received your letter, she insisted we post immediately to Town, and begged me to find out today whether you had yet arrived. She would have come herself, but the journey to Town has knocked her up."

"Poor Cindy could never travel easily."

Potton entered with a tray, and Lord Carfax accepted a glass of wine. His hostess also took one, feeling a little nervous of her visitor, who was studying her intently over the rim of his glass. As the butler closed the door behind him, Carfax spoke.

"You have not changed at all, Ros."

My lady inclined her head a little. "That is very kind of you, but I am a little older," she said softly.

"Are you well? Your letters have been all too rare. You should have contacted us as soon as you returned to England."

She smiled. "My apologies, Damien. I intended to write, but you know how it is, one keeps putting things off. But that is all past, I am here now."

"Do you intend to stay in Town long? I understand old Frencham left you his entire fortune. What will you do, sell the house?"

"No, I do not think I shall sell. I have taken a great fancy to this house, and I intend to stay here for a while before deciding what to do for the future."

"You should have known that if you wanted to stay in London, Cynthia and I would have been only too pleased to have you."

"It would not have worked," she interrupted him.

Carfax set down his empty glass on a small table beside him, saying in a low voice, "Cynthia thinks you have not forgiven her."

"There is nothing to forgive. It is merely that I prefer my own establishment."

He rose and went to the window, where he stood, staring out.

"That is not what will be said. They will think that old quarrels die hard."

"Then we must be sure that Cindy and I go about together frequently, although I doubt that anyone remembers what happened ten years ago. You refine too much upon the past, Damien. It is forgotten."

"I have not forgotten, Ros."

There was a pause, then Lady Rosalyn spoke in a low voice.

"It was very ill-judged of me to contract what was thought to be smallpox so soon after our engagement. Perhaps I should not have nursed Mama those last few weeks, but I cannot regret it, for I was a comfort to her."

"Please, Ros. If only you knew what it cost me."

"You were all so sure I would not recover, and that if I did I would be hideously marked."

Carfax stared unseeingly through the window. He said in an anguished tone, "I would have married you, Roasalyn. I did not ask you to break our engagement — I would never have done so."

Lady Rosalyn rose to her feet, clutching her glass tightly in her hands. She laughed mirthlessly.

"Very noble of you, sir, with Cynthia enacting a Cheltenham tragedy on one side, and you willing to be a martyr on the other. No, thank you! I had no wish for an unwilling husband!" She drew a breath, fighting down the anger and bitterness that had been suppressed for years. She continued quietly, "But that was ten years ago, Damien. You are now the father of a hopeful family, and I doubt not that you are happy."

He turned, rubbing a hand over his eyes.

"Sometimes, I think — " He looked searchingly at her. "And you, Rosalyn, are you happy?"

She turned away to place her glass beside his on the table.

"I am content."

She looked up, trying for a lighter note.

"Will you convey my love to my sister? Tell her I shall call on her tomorrow, if it is convenient."

She tugged at the bell-rope, and held out her hand. "Goodbye, Damien. We are brother and sister, you know; it is time we began to act as such. Ah, Potton, Lord Carfax is leaving. Will you show him out?"

Carfax took her hand, holding it for just a fraction longer than was necessary before departing without another word.

As the door closed behind him, Lady Rosalyn sank back in a chair.

She found that she was shaking, and closed her eyes for a moment, until the feeling of faintness had passed.

When Mrs. Windhurst entered the drawing-room some time later, she found her cousin sitting motionless, staring into space.

"Oh, Ros, I have had such an interesting morning! Only wait until you hear — Rosalyn my love! Whatever is the matter, have you been crying?" asked the widow, alarmed at the sight of tear-drops on my lady's cheek.

"What? Oh — no; just a silly dream, dearest, no more."

The following morning, Lady Rosalyn arrived at Carfax House to find her sister eagerly awaiting her in the Blue Salon. After a swift glance around the room, Rosalyn detected her sister's unerring eye for colour. The salon was decorated in pale blue and gilt, with everything in the first style of elegance. Lady Carfax was seated upon one of the small gilded sofas that were placed about the room. Lady Rosalyn smiled inwardly with appreciation. Her sister certainly had not forgotten how to show herself to advantage; she was dressed in a morning-gown of the palest blue, which matched her surroundings. Upon seeing her sister, Cynthia jumped up to embrace her.

"Oh, Rosalyn! Such a long time! How lovely you look."

Lady Carfax hugged her sister ruthlessly.

"Come and sit beside me, my love, and let me look at you."

Lady Rosalyn allowed herself to be guided to a sofa, and while she and Lady Carfax made themselves comfortable a footman arrived with a tray.

"You will take a dish of tea with me, will you not, Rosalyn? You were used to be quite fond of it, and I ordered it especially for you."

Touched by this kindness, Lady Rosalyn accepted the offer, saying, "How thoughtful of you, Cindy, thank you."

Lady Carfax looked searchingly at her sister.

"Damien told me you had not changed, Rosalyn, but you have. You are more beautiful than ever. In fact you look younger than I do, although you are more than a year older!"

Lady Rosalyn hid a smile at the note of petulance in her voice.

"Nonsense! You are still as pretty as ever!" she replied bracingly.

"But my figure!" wailed Lady Carfax comically. "Of course, after almost nine years of marriage and two children, one cannot expect to be as trim as one was, but I pride myself I am not an antidote! But enough of me: tell me your plans. Carfax tells me you intend to keep the house in Brook Street?"

"For the present, at least. I have not yet decided whether I would like to set up home here permanently. I am selling the country properties, with the exception of Larchwood, which is one of the smaller estates, and in need of attention my man of business informs

22

me. He thinks I shall get a good price for the rest."

"If you had informed me of your intention to visit Town, I would have invited you to stay with me."

"I did not know myself. It was clear that I could not remain with Harvey and Caroline for ever. Lord, what a bore he is turning out to be, Cindy. I thought I should die at times, for wanting to box his ears."

Cynthia giggled. "I know, my love! I felt the same when they were in Town last year. I do not know how Caroline can tolerate him."

"Well, she is even worse, always preaching propriety. When Mr. Frencham died, and left everything to me, it gave me just the excuse I needed to set up my own establishment without wounding their feelings. Do you know, Cynthia, Harvey was so pleased when he heard of the inheritance. I might find him a slow-top, but I must admit that he has my interests at heart."

"But the house is so large, surely you

will not live there alone, it would look so odd."

"But I am not alone. Amelia Windhurst is with me, and I do not doubt that Caroline will descend upon me should she wish to come to Town." Noting that Lady Carfax was looking rather anxious, she added, "I cannot see that anyone should object, there must be dozens of single gentlemen living in the same way, and no one minds in the least about them."

"Yes, but they live in their family homes, knowing that one day they will marry and bring their — " Cynthia broke off in confusion, waves of colour rushing to her cheeks.

There was an awkward silence before Lady Rosalyn spoke with an attempt at lightness.

"Well, who knows. It is not inconceivable that I should marry, even at my advanced age, although that is not my reason for coming to Town."

"Oh, Rosalyn, I am so sorry, I would not for the world — "

"Now, do you imagine me to be nursing a broken heart, or are you trying to convey the fact that I am much too old for marriage?" Rosalyn quizzed her gently. "I am sorry to disappoint you, Cindy, but my heart is quite intact, and if I remain single, it is through choice, not necessity, you know."

"But all these years! We have received so few letters from you."

"I am a very poor correspondent, my love, for that I apologise, but I beg you will not take it to mean that I bear you any grudge."

Lady Carfax dabbed at her eyes with a lace handkerchief, and exclaimed, "But you cannot deny that you loved him, Ros!"

"Perhaps I did once, but that was so very long ago, and if I have not seen you since then it is partly because I have been abroad for so long. When I returned to England — " she hesitated — "I admit I did not wish to descend upon you." Lady Rosalyn smiled a little wistfully at her sister. "It is quite an awkward situation, Cindy. Perhaps if we had seen more of each other after your marriage we could now be easy together. As it is — there will be talk of course. Old rumours will be unearthed, but once it is seen that we are all the best of friends, they will die quickly enough. It was ten years ago, and the fact that Carfax and I were once engaged can have no interest for the Ton today."

Lady Carfax listened in silence, tugging at her handkerchief. At last she spoke, saying somewhat defiantly, "He did love me, Ros, I could not give him up."

"I never asked you to, love. Perhaps that was because I never loved him so well as you. Are you afraid I have come back to stir up the coals? I assure you I have not, but I see no reason why I should be an exile from London."

"Oh no, of course not." Lady Carfax looked a little more cheerful. "It will be entertaining to introduce you to

London again, my dear. You cannot conceive how things have changed since you were last here. Carfax and I are going to the Coldridges tomorrow evening, and I will write them a note begging that I might bring you. Lady Coldridge is a good friend of mine, and I know she will not object."

"But Cynthia, I cannot possibly attend a ball so soon! I need to order more gowns and find my way around a little," replied Lady Rosalyn, laughing.

"I will furnish you with the addresses of all the best milliners and modistes in Town, Rosalyn, but for the Coldridges ball I am sure you have a suitable gown, for you have been to Brussels, and I am sure that the attire suitable for such august company as you kept there will not disgrace you here. Besides," added Lady Carfax naïvely, "it is very early in the season, and most of the Ton have not yet returned. It is to be quite a small affair, so you need not worry."

Lady Rosalyn was amused by her sister's conversation, and they spent a comfortable hour talking of the best warehouses to supply Lady Rosalyn with the materials for the many gowns she would need for the coming season. My lady left Carfax House with plenty to occupy her mind. It was obvious to her that Cynthia was worried. She smiled to herself a little. Had she looked older, a little more haggard, Cindy would have been less concerned, but it was apparent to Rosalyn that her sister, who had always had more hair than wit, was morbidly afraid that Damien, finding his first love unchanged by time, would also find her irresistible, especially as Lady Carfax had lost her girlhood bloom. She did not think that her sister had much to fear. From her brief and somewhat emotional meeting with Damien, she was fairly sure that his feelings for her were little more than a memory of what had been. For herself, well, time would tell, but Carfax had a wife and family to occupy him, and she would have to make certain that she gave him no opportunity to develop anything warmer for her than brotherly affection. The thought crossed her mind that it would be much easier to retire to the country, but she shook this off quickly. Why should she hide herself away from the world? The worst the Ton knew of her was that she had disobeyed her family and cried off from her engagement to Carfax, preferring to remain single. That was no crime, and her proud spirit rebelled from acting as if it were. No, Cynthia and Carfax would have to grow accustomed to her presence, for she would no longer give up her place in society for them.

2

LADY ROSALYN and her cousin spent the following morning visiting the fashionable modiste recommended by Cynthia. This lady proved to be very helpful, especially when she learned that her client was the sister of one of her most wealthy customers. As she emerged from the shop, Lady Rosalyn almost collided with another shopper. This lady was somewhat older than Rosalyn, but as she stepped back she gave a smile of recognition.

"Rosalyn, my dear! How delightful! But how long have you been in Town? I had quite given you up."

"Good morning, Lady Greenow. You know my cousin, Mrs. Windhurst, I believe?"

The two ladies greeted each other warmly, Mrs. Windhurst explaining to

Rosalyn that they had been presented together at Court many years ago. Lady Greenow turned again to Rosalyn.

"Well, Ros, what are you doing here? Do you stay with your sister?"

"No. I have my own house, in Brook Street — a legacy."

"Of course, old Frencham's place! I heard he had left it to you."

"I was his god-daughter, although I rarely saw him: he became something of a recluse in his later years, I believe. Amelia is residing with me for the present, to lend me countenance," added Rosalyn demurely.

Lady Greenow laughed delightedly.

"But this is wonderful news! I informed you when I saw you last that it was time you came to Town. That was in Brussels at the end of '15, do you remember? What an age ago that seems! I shall call upon you tomorrow, if I may — I have decided!"

Lady Rosalyn held out her hand, smiling warmly.

31

"We shall be delighted to receive you, ma'am."

Lady Greenow took her leave, and Mrs. Windhurst expressed her pleasure in the meeting, exclaiming that she was surprised the lady had remembered her, after all this time.

"She is so very good-natured, is she not, Amelia? She was unfailingly kind to me when Mama died — they were good friends you know — and in Brussels, whenever Aunt Farradae could not escort me to a party, she was always there to step in. I am delighted to have met her — it is a comfort to know that I have at least *one* acquaintance in Town."

"Does not Lord Greenow own estates adjoining Dowrings?"

Rosalyn nodded.

"Yes. After — Cynthia was wed and gone away, Lady Greenow came to Dowrings frequently to bear me company: she was one of the few people Papa would allow to come to the house. I do not know what I should have done without her support through those years."

They walked on in silence, Lady Rosalyn remembering the lonely months after her Mama's death, when she had cried off from her engagement to Damien. Her father had been furious, but not all his rantings could make her change her mind, and when he realised she would not be moved, he cut himself off from her, refusing to let her leave the estate, and allowing her few visitors. He spoke to her only to criticise, and from then to his death a few years later he never softened his attitude. The memory still held the power to chill Rosalyn, and she gave herself a mental shake. Amelia was aware of her cousin's changing emotions for they showed plainly on her countenance, but she could only guess at the cause. Lady Rosalyn had told no-one of her affection for Carfax, preferring the world to think her fickle. Only Damien and Cynthia knew the whole truth, although others who knew the sisters well drew their own conclusions.

Mrs. Windhurst thought perhaps she should make some comment to break the silence, but before she could speak Lady Rosalyn started upon some lighter topic, and the moment had passed.

Lady Greenow paid her promised visit the following day, and Lady Rosalyn was content to sit back as the two older ladies enjoyed a cosy chat about former times. The call ended with Lady Greenow promising to speak to her friend Lady Jersey about vouchers for Almacks, but Mrs. Windhurst forestalled her, swelling with pride a little as she informed her that they had met Maria Sefton and Lady Jersey at the Coldridge's ball the previous night, and Rosalyn's entrée to Almacks was already arranged.

Lady Rosalyn, a little apprehensive of attending her first engagement in London for nearly a decade, did justice to the occasion in a gown of amber silk, cut low at the neck and trimmed with cream lace. Beneath the flounced hem of her gown peeped new cream slippers, and to complete the toilet she wore her string of fine pearls, with matching drops in her ears. Her hair was dressed simply in curls, presenting such a charming picture that Mrs. Windhurst was able to report with satisfaction that she had received numerous compliments on the beauty of her companion.

The evening had begun a little less successfully with dinner at Carfax House. When they arrived, they found Lady Carfax awaiting them in the Blue Salon. Cynthia was attired in her favourite blue satin, and she wore the Carfax sapphires, a matching set of necklace and ear-rings, with a tiara nestled cunningly into her elegant coiffure. As she moved forward in a rustle of silken skirts to greet her guests, Lady Rosalyn exclaimed appreciatively, "You look magnificent, Cindy, those sapphires are perfect for you, they look as if they were chosen to match your eyes!"

"Thank you, Ros. You are looking very beautiful yourself." She turned to Mrs. Windhurst. "Amelia! What an age since we last met! You are looking very well, cousin."

Mrs. Windhurst smiled gratefully. She wore a gown of pale lavender, with a matching turban to cover her hair; she knew she was fortunate that the colours suitable for a widow should suit her so well. She glanced at her hostess.

"As always your taste is impeccable, Cynthia. But tell me, do you not think Rosalyn looks magnificent? She was afraid she would disgrace you by appearing like a country cousin."

The three ladies disposed themselves elegantly on the sofas close to the fire that blazed merrily to keep the chill spring air at bay. Lady Carfax surveyed her sister before replying to her cousin's remark.

"You need not fear that, Rosalyn," she said, somewhat wistfully, "you will outshine us all tonight."

Lady Rosalyn laughed. "What nonsense! I was always a foil to your fair beauty. It was indeed fortunate that I was not born fair, for with my lanky figure next to your own dainty form I would have had no admirers at all!" she exclaimed comically.

All three ladies laughed at this, and into this relaxed and jovial atmosphere entered Lord Carfax.

He greeted Mrs. Windhurst politely, and Lady Rosalyn took the opportunity to observe him. She had known a moment of shock when he entered, for she had forgotten quite how handsome he could look in satin knee-breeches and the tightly fitting dark coat he wore to such evening engagements. She noted that he was dressed with propriety, his neck-cloth tied to a nicety, and he wore no fobs or seals. His only ornament was a heavy gold signet-ring bearing the Carfax coat of arms. For a moment Rosalyn felt a great wave of despair rush over her for the past and what might have been. The next, Carfax was turning to her and she had to exert all her will power to greet him casually. There was no mistaking the look of admiration in his eyes when he looked at her, but her society manner did not desert her; knowing her sister's eyes to be upon them, she adopted a friendly if slightly distant manner. She could only be glad when the butler announced dinner, and was thankful to find her composure increasing as the meal progressed.

The evening turned out to be more enjoyable than Lady Rosalyn had expected. She was kindly received by her hostess, and was surprised to find she was remembered by so many of those present. Rosalyn was relieved when Carfax led his wife out to join the first set that was forming in the ballroom, and she spent a comfortable half-hour sitting with Mrs. Windhurst, who was able to point out most of the notables present. She danced once with her brother-in-law, during which time she refused to be drawn into any conversation other than the most unexceptional topics, and could only be glad when he took himself off to the card-room for the rest of the evening. Rosalyn could not but feel that his eyes followed her too often, and she knew her own countenance to be more flushed than usual.

When they arrived home in the early hours of the morning, Mrs. Windhurst made her way to her cousin's room, where Rosalyn was preparing for bed. Mrs. Windhurst declared herself well satisfied with the evening.

"You were a hit, my dear! A success! Oh, you have no idea how many people asked me who you were, or commented upon how well you looked. And when you told me that Lady Jersey had agreed to send you vouchers for Almacks, I could have died of happiness!"

Lady Rosalyn looked at her cousin, amused.

"Does it really mean so much to you, Amelia — my success?"

"But of course! I have known you since you were a little child, you were the daughter I never had, Ros, and nothing gives me greater pleasure than your happiness," replied Mrs. Windhurst simply.

Lady Rosalyn crossed the room to hug her ruthlessly.

"You are the best of cousins, then!"

"You will see how sought after you will be, my love. The invitations will come pouring in. Oh, you will break hearts, my dear, I know it!" the widow exclaimed in a rapturous tone.

Lady Rosalyn paused from brushing her hair. "I have no wish to break hearts, Amelia. I would lief make friends and live comfortably here as a single lady," she said quietly.

Keeping her reflections to herself, Mrs. Windhurst returned a non-committal answer and went off to bed.

The evening had been less successful for Lady Carfax. She had been aware of her husband's look of admiration when he had first seen Rosalyn, and she felt a cold fear within her. Cynthia had never known Carfax to pay attention to any woman other than herself, and she had come to take his attentions for granted. That night, however, was very different. Damien appeared distracted, and when he led his sister-in-law out to join a set later in the evening, Cynthia had difficulty in attending to her companion for she found her eyes constantly returning to the dancers. Mrs. Cartside, while keeping up a flow of conversation was not slow to perceive my lady's inattention, and after a time she paused, letting her own eyes follow Cynthia's to where Lady Rosalyn and Carfax were moving down the dance. She sighed audibly.

"What a pleasure it is to have Lady Rosalyn with us again. I vow she is as beautiful as ever." She threw a sidelong glance at Cynthia. "No doubt you are delighted to have her with you again."

"We are indeed," came the quiet reply.

Mrs. Cartside watched the couple on the dance-floor for a few moments, and commented slyly, "They dance so well together, do they not, and make such a striking pair — so tall as they both are!"

To her own annoyance, Cynthia felt a flush come to her cheeks, but she returned calmly, "My sister was always a most graceful dancer."

Lady Carfax then moved away, inwardly seething. There could be no mistaking the meaning behind Mrs. Cartside's words. The woman had a nose for scandal, and she plainly remembered the betrothal between Rosalyn and Carfax. Cynthia's pleasure in the evening was destroyed, and even when Carfax moved off into the adjoining salon where Lord Coldridge had set up card-tables, she could not be easy. Cynthia observed her sister, making her way amongst the crowd. Her years abroad had given her poise and elegance, and she conversed easily with her acquaintance.

Lady Carfax wished that her sister had not returned to Town, but an instant later she was ashamed of herself for such thoughts, and she turned hastily away, resolved to leave the ballroom and go in search of Mrs. Windhurst. A voice at her shoulder halted her.

"Your pardon, ma'am — yours I believe?"

Cynthia looked around to find herself confronting a gentleman unknown to her. He was holding up an ivory fan.

"Oh yes. It is mine." Lady Carfax bestowed a slight smile upon him. "I thank you, sir."

"I am pleased to have been of service — Lady Carfax."

"Have we been introduced, sir?" Lady Carfax looked puzzled. "I regret I do not recall — "

"Unfortunately not, my lady. I am an old friend of your sister — it was she who pointed you out to me." He made her an elegant bow. "Richard Stayne, at your service, ma'am."

My lady relaxed a little, and gave him the tips of her fingers.

"No doubt you became acquainted with Lady Rosalyn abroad, sir?" she enquired as he raised her hand to his lips. His hair, she noted idly, was as fair as her own.

"Indeed, ma'am, that is so; an enchanting lady — " He hesitated.

"Are you perhaps otherwise engaged, Lady Carfax, or will you allow me to procure a little refreshment for?"

Cynthia hesitated, but his next words persuaded her, for he confided with a smile that he knew so few of the guests who were present. "Having only recently returned to England."

"Then I shall take pity upon you," laughed Cynthia.

Later that night, when travelling back to Carfax House with her husband, Cynthia recalled the half-hour spent in the company of her new acquaintance as the most enjoyable of the whole evening. Mr. Stayne was a man of obvious charm, and clearly practised in the art of pleasing. He had flattered her in a most subtle manner, making her feel that he considered her to be the most attractive lady in the room. Of course, she could not take such a gentleman seriously, but it was refreshing to be treated thus, and she was not averse to furthering her acquaintance with Mr. Stayne.

3

MRS. WINDHURST'S prediction turned out to be true: Lady Rosalyn could not but be flattered by the number of invitations that she received after the Coldridge Ball. Many were from matrons with sons of marriageable age, but there were also many from those who remembered her from her previous sojourn in Town, besides a good number from friends she had made abroad.

Lady Rosalyn was pleased at the way she had been accepted by the Ton, although she knew enough of the world to guess that the Frencham fortune had contributed no small part to her success. One or two remarks had reached her that convinced her there were some malicious enough to rake up the past, and it strengthened her resolve to be seen to be on the best of terms with both her sister and brother-in-law. To this end it was arranged that Lady Rosalyn and her cousin should join Lord Carfax's party on a trip to Vauxhall Gardens. Lady Rosalyn had heard so much of the gardens, but had never visited them, and she found herself looking forward to the event. To add to the entertainment, it was agreed that they should attend the masquerade night, Lady Carfax assuring her sister that there could be nothing improper about such an evening, since Damien would be escorting them. Cynthia presented her sister with a cherry-red domino that she had never worn, for although it had seemed perfect when she had first seen it at Madam Sophie's, Cynthia had realised as soon as she got it home that the colour was not right for her. Lady Rosalyn accepted the gift gratefully, and when she put the domino around her shoulders, together with the loo mask to complete the effect, she felt a thrill of excitement.

Everything went according to plan, and the party met at Carfax House in readiness for the evening's entertainment. Besides Lady Rosalyn, her cousin and Lord and Lady Carfax, the party consisted of Sir Timothy Marchant, an elderly widower whom Lady Carfax had invited on impulse when she discovered he had a decided partiality for Mrs. Windhurst, and to keep the numbers even, she had invited a single gentleman, Mr. Bradley: he was something of a rattle, but she hoped he would amuse Lady Rosalyn. Everyone was determined to be pleased, and the party set off for Vauxhall in high spirits.

Lord Carfax had hired a box for the evening, where supper would be taken later in the evening. From here they could watch the dancing which was in progress and listen to the orchestra. Lady Rosalyn's enjoyment of the spectacle was marred by the fact that Mr. Bradley, who had attached himself particularly to her, was drinking steadily. She did not doubt that she could handle the situation should his flirtatious manner get out of hand, but she thought that Lady Carfax could have provided her with a more entertaining partner for the evening. Rosalyn was also aware that Damien was watching her, and she felt it would be better for all concerned if she removed herself from the proximity of her brother-in-law. To this end, she suggested to Mr. Bradley that they should take a stroll about the gardens, for she had not yet had a chance to study the thousands of lamps that lighted the paths. Mr. Bradley rose with alacrity. He had been disappointed to find that his companion was a very cool young lady with no inclination to flirt with him, and her proposal came as a very pleasant surprise: he concluded that she had been a little shy at first, and he was not unhopeful of a little dalliance before the night was out.

Lady Rosalyn was glad for the

protection of the mask and domino, for her companion seemed to sway slightly as they walked. Lost in her own thoughts, she let her escort lead her through the paths, where a number of couples were to be seen, marvelling at the ingenious lanterns that were hung up to light the way. Before long, Lady Rosalyn realised that they had left the main pathway and were heading along a much more secluded walk. She wondered if this was wise, and was about to suggest that they turn back when her escort stole an arm around her waist: she felt his mouth close to her ear.

"Now, my dear, perhaps I can steal a kiss before we return to the others."

She twisted out of his grasp.

"How dare you, sir! I do not know what you expected, but I am sure Lord Carfax would not approve of your behaviour!"

"Oh, Damien is an old woman when it comes to the ladies," he said obscurely, and leaned towards her. "You cannot be so cruel as to refuse me a kiss, was not that why you wished to walk alone with me?"

"It most certainly was not! We will return immediately, Mr. Bradley!"

"Not so fast, my lady," he slurred his words as he moved forward to grasp her arm, and Rosalyn dealt him a ringing slap.

"Enough of this foolery, sir! I take leave to tell you that I find your behaviour ignominious and extremely distasteful. I warn you if you do not remove yourself from my presence this minute I will have no option but to inform my brother-in-law how you abuse his hospitality." She saw in the dim light that he was looking a little abashed, and continued less severely, "I suggest you make your way home, and I will make your apologies to my sister."

Realising he had mistaken the lady, Mr. Bradley bowed unsteadily. "As you wish, ma'am. I beg your pardon."

"Yes, well, we will forget this matter,

51

if you please. Perhaps the next time we meet you will have remembered your manners."

"Your servant, ma'am."

With another shaky bow, he set off along the path and was soon out of sight. Lady Rosalyn gave a sigh of relief.

"Bravo, ma'am."

She jumped, and turned to see who had spoken. A large dark shape detached itself from the shadows; instinctively she moved back a pace towards the one dim lantern that was burning in that part of the gardens.

"You certainly sent him about his business, my dear, a masterly set-down."

"If you will excuse me, sir, I must return to my party," she replied coldly.

"But you must allow me to escort you." The stranger barred her way. "It is not safe for a young lady to wander alone through these paths. One never knows whom one might meet."

"Thank you, sir, but that will not be necessary."

She stepped aside, but again he was in front of her. It was an awkward situation, but my lady was not afraid. She appraised the stranger quickly. He was tall, well above average height, with thick dark hair above a long, lean face. There were deep lines at the sides of his mouth, accentuated by the shadows, and through the slits of his mask his eyes glittered eerily. She guessed from his apparel that he was a member of her own world; he wore a dark domino, but where it fell open at the front she could make out an elaborate waistcoat, light-coloured pantaloons and a pair of shining Hessians, sporting gold tassels. Clearly a man of quality, but how dangerous he was she could not tell, for they were in a secluded spot, and she had already had to deal with one member of the Quality! The gentleman folded his arms, regarding her with a slight, mocking smile.

"Well, ma'am, do I pass inspection?"

"You are certainly *dressed* as a gentleman, but I do not know that I can rely on you to act as one," she replied frankly.

The stranger laughed, revealing white, even teeth.

"But how can I behave as a gentleman when you refuse to let me escort you?"

"You may stand aside, sir. I should be most grateful for that."

"What? And let such beauty walk out of my life? First we must be better acquainted: pray honour me with your name."

The idea that he had been drinking crossed her mind, and she glanced about her quickly. They were not far from a well-lighted path: if she could reach that, she would be safer. Lady Rosalyn moved swiftly to one side in an attempt to brush past the stranger, but he was quicker, and she found herself pinned tightly to him, his strong hands firmly holding her arms behind her. She found herself thinking in a detached way how tall he was. Being tall herself, Lady Rosalyn was not accustomed to look up at a man.

"Now, my mysterious beauty, your name."

"How dare you!" Her eyes sparkled angrily through the slits of her mask. "Let me go at once!"

"Only tell me your name, my dear. You must be new to Town. I would not have forgotten such a one had we met," he mused.

"Nor I you!" she flashed, struggling against his vice-like grip. Realising it was useless, she paused, saying scornfully, "You cannot keep me here for ever. Someone will come along and you will have to let me go."

"Only tell me your name, fair one, and you shall be freed."

Lady Rosalyn hesitated: she had no wish to prolong this encounter.

"Very well. But you must release me a little first. I can scarce breathe."

Her captor stepped back a little, releasing one of her wrists.

"As you wish, ma'am."

She drew herself up, stating in her haughtiest tone, "I am Lady Rosalyn Tremayne. Now, release me, if you please!"

Ignoring this request, he regarded her thoughtfully.

"Tremayne? Old Percy Tremayne's daughter? I thought she was a yellow-haired chit, married to Carfax."

"That is my sister."

With a quick movement he flicked off her mask, studying her face intently.

"Then why have I not seen you in Town?"

Lady Rosalyn curbed her impatience, and explained. "I have been abroad, sir. Now, I demand you let me go!"

"Oho! You demand, my beauty? And what terrible fate awaits me if I do not comply? Is there some lover to call me out?"

She lowered her eyes, saying in a low tone, "There is no-one. You must be aware that my father is dead, and I have no brothers to protect me. I rely on your good breeding."

She looked up at him, meeting his glance squarely as he replied, a little bitterly, "I should not rely too heavily upon that, my dear."

Lady Rosalyn detected the sound of voices: someone was approaching from another pathway. She looked at her assailant triumphantly. His head was thrown back, listening, then before she could protest, he pulled her to him, kissing her soundly.

"Infamous fiend!" exclaimed Lady Rosalyn when he released her.

He pulled her arm through his, still retaining his grip so that it was impossible for her to pull away.

"I was overset by your beauty, my lady." He handed her the loo mask. "You had best replace this before I am overwhelmed once more."

He released her arm, and my lady did as she was bid. She bit her lip, saying sternly, "You are ridiculous, sir."

"Nay, ma'am," he returned piously,

"a woman of such outstanding radiance should not be allowed to go about in public, for have you not witnessed this very night the devastating effect you have on mere mortals?"

Ignoring the choking sound from his companion, he once more pulled her hand through his arm and led her towards the main pathway.

"Now, my lady, if you will show me the direction of your party I shall endeavour to restore you to them safely. There are some most undesirable characters lurking in these gardens, you know."

"I am well aware of that," replied my lady meaningfully. She glanced up at him curiously. "What *were* you doing alone in those gardens? Do you make it a habit to lie in wait for defenceless females?"

"I was in fact enjoying a cigarillo, before I was compelled to come to your rescue."

"Of all the — You did not rescue me!" exclaimed Lady Rosalyn wrathfully.

"In fact, I feel I should have been much safer had I remained with Mr. Bradley."

"Perhaps, but he would not have made you laugh, now would he?" he argued.

Rosalyn was obliged to choke back another gurgle of laughter, and she maintained a haughty silence until they approached the box where the rest of the party, with the exception of Mr. Bradley, were about to partake of a champagne supper. At the sight of Lady Rosalyn and her escort, Lady Carfax gave a slight shriek.

"Ros! Where is Mr. Bradley?"

Ros realised from the look of cold hauteur that Cynthia bestowed upon her escort that she was not pleased with his presence. Her companion seemed completely unaware of this animosity, however, replying to Lady Carfax's question in the blandest way.

"Mr. Bradley was — ah — taken ill during the walk, my lady, and as he was unable to accompany Lady

Rosalyn back to you, I undertook to see her safely restored." He added, glancing at the silent figure beside him, "You know, Carfax, I fear Mr. Bradley had been imbibing a little too freely? I do not think he is a fitting companion for your sister, do you?"

Lord Carfax ignored this remark, turning his attention to Lady Rosalyn. "I trust you have not been inconvenienced, Lady Rosalyn?"

The meaning of this was all too clear, but Rosalyn had no wish to be the means of a quarrel, and disclaimed. She entered the box and joined her sister at the table, while her erstwhile escort made his bow to the assembled company.

"Thank you for your offer, Carfax, but I cannot stay to dine. I must join my own party, you know. I have already been away far too long."

"Well!" exclaimed Lady Carfax as she watched the tall, lanky figure saunter away. "What impudence! I was never more shocked in my life than when I saw you walk up on his arm."

"No — were you so alarmed? Then you must tell me his name, for I did not discover it."

Lady Carfax stared at her in amazement.

"Do you tell me that you have been walking in the gardens with a gentleman who has not been introduced to you? That, dear Rosalyn, was Rake Hellborn!" She saw the blank look on her sister's face, and lowered her voice a little, to explain, "Sir Marcus Helston, and considered to be one of the most dangerous rakes in London! He has not a feather to fly with, you know, so I cannot feel that it is an acquaintance you should pursue."

Lady Rosalyn looked amused.

"It is not I who would wish to pursue it!" she said, and putting the matter out of her head she turned her attention to the supper laid out before her.

As they drove home after taking their leave of Lord and Lady Carfax, Mrs.

Windhurst repeated to Lady Rosalyn the wisdom of keeping wolves such as Sir Marcus at bay.

"There is no doubt, my love, that he is a profligate, and I should hate to see you fall into his clutches."

"What a pity you were not present when Mr. Bradley took his leave, Amelia, for you could then have defended me from this rake."

Mrs. Windhurst gasped. "Ros, my love! Never tell me he took advantage of you! Why did you not tell Carfax, he would have known how to deal with the villain."

Lady Rosalyn blushed in the darkness. "You must see how impossible it would be for me to tell Damien. He would have been only too pleased to pick a quarrel, and what a story that would lead to. Besides, it was not so very bad, I returned to you unscathed from my encounter," she replied mendaciously, and in the darkness her fingers crept to her sore wrist. It was most likely that she would have a fine bruise there tomorrow, and she gave mental thanks for the current fashion for long sleeves.

A week later, the marks were still evident, although they were fading, as Lady Rosalyn noted with relief as she adjusted the cuffs of her gown. She had not seen her assailant since their encounter at Vauxhall, and she was aware that Lady Carfax was concerned that they might see him at the Greenow's party that evening.

"All the world and his wife will be present, my love," Cynthia informed her sister. "It will be the most shocking squeeze! Sir Ingram is distantly related to that odious creature who accosted you at Vauxhall, Ros, and it is most likely that he will be there."

Lady Rosalyn was amused at her sister's concern.

"Do you think I should cry off, then? Perhaps I could plead a headache."

"No, no. You must go. You need not speak to him, after all, for you have not been introduced — but I think it is best that are forewarned."

A slight smile touched Rosalyn's lips as she recalled those words: Cindy was treating her as though she had just left the schoolroom, with no notion of how to go on! She looked up as her maid entered.

"The carriage is awaiting you, my lady. Mrs. Windhurst asked me to tell you she will meet you downstairs."

Lady Rosalyn cast a final appraising glance into the mirror, twitched her silk shawl a little more becomingly across her arms, and set off to join her cousin.

When they arrived at the Greenow's imposing residence in Piccadilly, Lady Rosalyn's first impression was that the house was overflowing with guests. Lady Greenow, looking triumphant, beamed down at them as they ascended the grand staircase towards her.

"My dears, I had all but given you up! You look radiant, as usual, Rosalyn. Sir Ingram will be so pleased you have come."

"I am amazed that you should have missed us in this throng!" smiled Rosalyn.

Lady Greenow gave a tinkling laugh. "I know, my dear, — is it not gratifying?" She gazed around her. "I am sure it is the biggest squeeze of the season! Everyone is here, and there is one I know who is particularly anxious to see you here!" Her eyes twinkled merrily. "Major Franklyn," she whispered.

"Oh dear!" Lady Rosalyn turned to her cousin. "Amelia, pray do not leave my side tonight!" she begged.

"But who is this admirer?" asked Mrs. Windhurst, greatly intrigued.

"He is a most gallant soldier," said Lady Greenow, before Rosalyn could reply. "He has been striving to win the affections of this most ungrateful lady for I don't know how many years! It has been rumoured," she continued in a confidential tone, "that he was spurred on by his affections to courageous action at Quatre Bras!"

Lady Rosalyn laughed. "Amelia, I beg you will not listen! I have tried my best to discourage the Major!"

As the attention of their hostess was claimed at that moment by the arrival of more guests, Mrs. Windhurst moved on into the ballroom with her cousin.

"I am anxious to meet this suitor, Ros!"

"Then I am sure you will have the opportunity tonight. I am also convinced he will meet your notions of what is proper in a suitor, for he is a most worthy gentleman."

Although she chuckled to herself, Rosalyn would say no more, and they made their way across to a less crowded corner of the room, stopping frequently on their way to exchange greetings with acquaintances. Lady Rosalyn's attention was soon claimed by an urgent whisper from her cousin.

"Ros! That creature is here."

"What creature, my love?"

"Over there, flirting with Lady Murchiston — the lady in the yellow gown — it is Sir Marcus!"

"Surely not, Amelia! Sir Marcus could never be female, and I am sure he would not wear — "

Mrs. Windhurst rapped her knuckles with her fan, saying severely, "You wilfully misunderstand me, Rosalyn! I mean he is talking with the lady in the yellow gown!"

Lady Rosalyn followed her cousin's outraged glance to a distant alcove, where a voluptuous blonde, whom Rosalyn took to be Lady Murchiston, was laughing up at a very tall gentleman at her side.

That is Rake Hellborn then, she thought. Without the mask he looked younger, his lean face less harsh, although he could not be called handsome. His hair was dark, and cut almost unfashionably short. There was a careless elegance about his dress, and although the dark blue coat became him well, it was not moulded to his form, and his cravat was negligently tied: for all that,

Lady Rosalyn thought him a striking figure.

"My dear, you have not listened to one word!"

Lady Rosalyn started from her reverie, turned to her cousin and gave her a rueful smile.

"Your pardon, Amelia — what said you?"

Mrs. Windhurst shook her head, laughing. "It matters not, Ros, except that there is a gentleman approaching."

Lady Rosalyn cast an imploring glance at her cousin.

"It is Major Franklyn! Amelia, I beg you, do not desert me!"

The gentleman in question stood before the two ladies and made his bow. He took Lady Rosalyn's hand and raised it reverently to his lips.

"My dear Lady Rosalyn!" He gazed up at her earnestly. "Your beauty overwhelms me, ma'am. I have never seen its equal."

"Thank you Major. Let me introduce you to my cousin, Mrs. Windhurst: she is staying with me at present."

Again the stately bow. He turned again to Lady Rosalyn.

"I had heard you were living in Brook Street," he said in measured tones. "I admit, it is not what one could like for a lady of your gentle breeding to live alone in such a way, but we must hope that it will not be for a long duration."

"Must we?"

Mrs. Windhurst, recognising the sparkle of anger in her cousin's eyes, intervened hastily.

"Do you have your own house in Town, Major?"

"No, ma'am. My mother and I spend very little time in the metropolis, and it would be an extravagance to set up an establishment here — I have taken up residence at the Clarendon."

"Is it to be a long stay?" inquired Mrs. Windhurst.

"Mama wishes to remove to Worthing later in the season, but first she is hopeful of making your acquaintance,

Lady Rosalyn: I have told her so much about you, she tells me she feels she knows you already."

"I hope you have not made me out to be a paragon, sir," remarked Rosalyn.

"No, no. I have described you to her very faithfully, I believe, although one must allow for a certain prejudice on my part." He smiled, and looked meaningfully at Lady Rosalyn, who chose to ignore the innuendo.

"How kind you are, Major! I shall be delighted to meet Mrs. Franklyn. Oh! I have seen someone I simply must speak with, so perhaps you will entertain my cousin for me, Major, while I am away," Lady Rosalyn smiled sunnily at Amelia. "I am sure you will enjoy a most interesting chat. My cousin," continued Rosalyn, lowering her voice, "is convinced that one of the gentleman present is in reality a female."

"Rosalyn!" cried Mrs. Windhurst, turning pink.

Lady Rosalyn laughed and walked

away, leaving her cousin to gaze after her in indignation.

"Such an admirable creature!" Major Franklyn sighed audibly.

"Apart from her sense of humour!" remarked Mrs. Windhurst, hoping the blush had now left her cheeks.

"Ah, you think I shall be offended by her little jokes, Mrs. Windhurst, but I assure you that is not the case! I hope I am well enough acquainted with Lady Rosalyn to overlook this tiny flaw in her character, and I am sure that if she were to have the benefit of my Mama's counsel for any length of time, these odd humours could be eradicated."

Mrs. Windhurst looked at the speaker in astonishment.

"Oh, I know what you are thinking," said the Major with a little laugh, "You are saying to yourself, there is a man deeply in love. And it is true, Mrs. Windhurst, I believe that in Lady Rosalyn I have discovered the perfect soul-mate, the ideal companion for life's long voyage, one whom I should feel honoured to protect against the contrary winds of life!"

Unfortunately for the Major, his auditor could not agree, and after making a non-committal reply, Mrs. Windhurst made good her escape.

When she later came upon Lady Rosalyn, Mrs. Windhurst was quick to reprimand her for her conduct earlier that evening.

"Such rag-manners, Rosalyn, to leave me with the Major in such a way!"

"I beg your pardon, Amelia, but when he took it into his head to criticise my life-style, I was sorely tempted to give him a sharp set-down."

"I could see you were angry, love, but you should not be so harsh; the Major blatantly adores you. In fact," said Mrs. Windhurst, an irrepressible bubble of laughter in her voice, "he wishes to protect you from the contrary winds of life."

"Good God, did he say that?" exclaimed Lady Rosalyn in horrified accents, then she smiled mischievously.

"At my age I should be grateful for such an admirer, should I not? But such is my perversity that I wish he could be persuaded to fall in love with someone else!"

Lady Rosalyn and her cousin soon separated, for although their acquaintance in Town was not large, it was sufficient to allow them to move about the rooms freely. Lady Greenow came upon Lady Rosalyn as the floor was clearing for the first dance of the evening, and she smiled at her young friend, her round face a little flushed with the heat.

"Alone, Rosalyn? I trust you are enjoying yourself tonight."

"Thank you, ma'am, very much. I congratulate you on your success."

Lady Greenow beamed more than ever.

"Indeed, it is a fair start to the season," she said modestly. She turned her bright, merry face towards Lady Rosalyn, saying in an undertone, "I was about to suggest that I introduce you to one of the gentlemen for the first dance, but I can see that one is about to ask you to stand up with him."

Glancing over her shoulder, Lady Rosalyn saw Major Franklyn making his way purposefully towards them. She laid her hand on her hostess's arm, saying in mock despair, "Then I am lost! Pray stay beside me, Lady Greenow! Let us say I do not dance tonight!"

Lady Greenow merely smiled and patted her arm.

"Nonsense!" she said, moving away. "You will enjoy yourself, Rosalyn, that is why you are here!"

Left to meet the Major, Lady Rosalyn could do nothing but accept his invitation to dance with good grace, and they walked out to join the set. During the dance, the conversation seemed to Lady Rosalyn to consist of inane platitudes, and by the end of the movement she was heartily bored with her sober companion. The Major was but a few years older than herself, but he had been responsible for his family from his twentieth year, when his father had died suddenly. He was not one to shirk his duty, but it had aged him considerably. His mother had insisted that he continue his career with the army, but although his temperament made him painstakingly thorough in his duties, he lacked the initiative required to make a great soldier. He had been attached to Wellington's staff during 1815, and Rosalyn was acquainted with most of his colleagues: she was aware that they made fun of his sober character, and they had viewed his ponderous but determined pursuit of her with hilarity, but thankfully for Lady Rosalyn, the novelty of the joke soon palled, and they ignored the Major altogether. Even this did not affect him, for his own self-esteem prevented him from feeling any slight, and Rosalyn, realising that most of her snubs went unnoticed by her admirer, felt very little compunction for avoiding him whenever possible.

When the dance was over, Major

Franklyn led his partner to a vacant chair and walked off to procure a glass of lemonade for the lady. Rosalyn glanced quickly around the crowded room, her eyes searching for Mrs. Windhurst, or some other ally, but could find none. She wished that her acquaintance in Town were greater, for in Brussels there had always been some young officer willing to lead her on to the dance-floor when she had had enough of the Major's attentions. A voice behind her chair made her jump.

"What a pleasure it is to see you again, ma'am."

She turned her head to see Sir Marcus Helston standing behind her.

"We have not been introduced, sir," she said in arctic tones.

"No, we introduced ourselves, did we not, Lady Rosalyn?"

Sir Marcus moved round to sit beside her

"I wonder you have the effrontery to mention that episode!"

76

"Oh, I have no proper feeling, I assure you," he replied blandly. He watched her, a slight smile curving his lips. "You can scarcely say that you do not know me, ma'am, when your cousin so obligingly pointed me out to you."

Her eyes flew to his face. Seeing her surprise, his smile grew.

"You were going to pretend you had no idea who I was, is that it? How uncharitable!"

"But not so uncharitable as you, to force your attentions upon me!" she retorted bitterly.

"My dear girl, do you expect me to believe that you are not bored to tears by that slow-top, and praying for someone to rescue you?"

Lady Rosalyn was about to make a sharp retort when she thought of the Major returning with her glass of lemonade, and the truth of Sir Marcus' words struck home. She remained silent. Sir Marcus spoke again.

"I understand you are residing in Brook Street with your cousin."

She inclined her head a little.

"It will give me great pleasure to call upon you," he murmured, his eyes on her profile.

At his words she turned an indignant face towards him.

"Useless, sir! You would not be welcome at my house!"

"Do you know," he replied, "your eyes are the most charming colour, and they are magnificent when you are angry!"

"You are absurd, Sir Marcus!" she said severely. "I see the Major is returning, so there is no need for you to remain."

Sir Marcus did indeed rise from his seat, but he made no attempt to move away, merely swinging his eyeglass very gently to and fro on its ribbon.

Major Franklyn presented the lemonade to Rosalyn with a flourish.

"My apologies for the delay, Lady Rosalyn, it was not my intention to abandon you for so long." As he spoke the Major cast a glance at Sir Marcus that was so full of disapproval Lady Rosalyn was hard pressed not to laugh.

She said affably, "No matter, Major. May I present Sir Marcus Helston to you, sir?"

"No need, my dear! The Major and I have been acquainted for many a year!" interrupted Sir Marcus jovially.

"A very distant acquaintance, I assure you, ma'am," said Major Franklyn heavily.

Sir Marcus smiled at his adversary.

"If you recall, Lady Rosalyn, you have promised me the next dance. If you are ready, ma'am?"

Lady Rosalyn hesitated. She was in an awkward situation: she knew she ought to refuse — impertinent creature, that would make him look no-how! But she was aware that if she did, she would be obliged to stay with the Major, and the thought of another half-hour of dull conversation was almost unbearable.

As though he read her thoughts, Sir Marcus smiled down at her and held out his hand.

"Just so, Lady Rosalyn," he said softly.

She laughed a little, putting her hand out to him, and saying to the Major as she rose, "Indeed he is right, sir. I am afraid I must go — my lemonade must wait for my return."

During the first few minutes of the dance, Lady Rosalyn maintained what she hoped was a dignified reserve, returning only monosyllabic answers to the unexceptional remarks put to her by her partner. He did not appear to be in the least discomposed, but after a while he remarked, looking down at her in amusement,

"Do you know, Lady Rosalyn, I cannot but believe that if you were to try just a little harder, you might enjoy yourself."

"You deserve that I should have exposed your impertinence before Major Franklyn, and refused to stand up with you!" retorted Lady Rosalyn.

Sir Marcus put up his brows. "Are you telling me that you are dancing with me merely to save my face? What a bouncer! I am well aware that you accepted my invitation to escape from your prosy admirer!"

This was so close to the truth that Lady Rosalyn was forced to laugh, and she was thankful that the dance separated them at that point, so that she was able to recover her icy reserve.

4

REMEMBERING his words, Lady Rosalyn gave orders the following morning that should Sir Marcus call, she was not at home. However, her precautions proved unnecessary, for when she enquired of Potton at dinnertime if any gentleman had called, the reply was negative. Rosalyn felt a little disappointed but gave herself a mental shake, acknowledging that after the fulsome compliments he had paid her, she was a little piqued he had made no attempt to see her.

Sir Marcus had in fact no opportunity to call, for he received that morning a note from an ageing aunt commanding him to attend her. The Dowager Duchess of Kendle lived some twenty-five miles south of London, on the Tonbridge road, and Sir Marcus, driving himself in his curricle, arrived there soon after noon. He slowed his team and turned them into the drive leading up to the house — an imposing residence built on a slight rise and commanding excellent views of the surrounding country. An ancient retainer was waiting at the door, and he showed Sir Marcus to a cosy, panelled apartment on the first floor, where the Dowager Duchess was waiting. She was seated in a large armchair, dressed in her habitual black, with her white hair covered by a black lace cap. She reminded Sir Marcus forcibly of a bird of prey, and it was no surprise to him that the lady's family were terrified of her. He showed no signs of discomfiture as he entered, merely returning her frosty glare with the blandest of smiles.

"I expected you a good hour ago, Marcus!"

He bowed gracefully, and lifted her thin hand to his lips.

"Alas, your Grace, my time-keeping is abominable."

The lady gave a cackling laugh, her stern features relaxing a little.

"Well, at least you do not offer me timorous excuses like the rest of my brood. Sit down, boy. I can't talk while you tower over me!"

Unperturbed, Sir Marcus lowered his long frame into a chair close to his hostess.

"Well, ma'am, to what do I owe the honour of your invitation?"

"I want to talk to you. I hear you are playing deep these days."

Sir Marcus looked surprised.

"I have been doing so for years, ma'am, but how it should have come to your ears — "

"Oh, I am very well informed of what's abroad, never fear. I am concerned for you, Marcus," she replied, adding in an unladylike way, "I'm damned if I know why I should be, for a greater care-for-nobody I have yet to meet!"

"Alas, ma'am, I am told it comes from my father's family."

"Hah! You mean myself, I suppose! Well, that could be true, but in my day we did not have such namby-pamby notions of what was improper. I can't abide these modern ways: take Celia, Kendle's wife, for instance."

"I had much rather not," murmured her nephew, grimacing.

The Dowager threw him a scornful glance. "Can't say a word to that girl without she bursts into tears or has an attack of the vapours. Too mealy-mouthed, these young women of today." The Dowager paused, considering this statement. Sir Marcus prompted her gently.

"I fear we stray from the point, your Grace."

"What's that? Oh, yes. Very well, Marcus, I know that your estates are mortgaged to the hilt, and you have run through your fortune until you are almost at a stand."

"Your pardon, ma'am, my fortune, as you call it, was almost gone before I inherited it."

"I don't deny that your father wasted his blunt a little too freely, Marcus, but with a little economy you could have brought yourself about. Instead of that you are running yourself into the ground."

"Well, and if I am? That concerns no-one but myself."

"Now don't get on your high horse with me, my boy, for I am much too old to take a set-down from you!"

Sir Marcus relaxed a little, smiling.

"Indeed, your Grace, I am sure you would annihilate me with one of your scolds if I should attempt to do such a thing."

The Dowager looked pleased with this tribute, and she continued in a milder tone, "The reason I have called you here is to strike a bargain."

"A bargain, ma'am. What can you want of me?"

"It is time you were settling down, Marcus. I am considering changing my will — in fact my lawyer is calling on me this very day for that purpose."

She saw the look of surprise on his face, and continued gruffly, "I have decided that I shall leave my fortune to you, on condition that you make a respectable marriage and give up your rake-hell ways. Oh yes, my boy, I know that you are called Hellborn in Town, and I know too that the latest female you are keeping must be costing you much more than you can afford."

Sir Marcus gave an involuntary laugh.

"You never fail to surprise me, my dear aunt! I have thought I was accountable to none, but it seems you have me under constant surveillance."

"I like to know what is going on in the world, no more. Now what do you say?" she urged him. "Once it is known that you will one day have my fortune, a respectable alliance is not impossible. I do not say that it can be a brilliant match, for you have led far too wild a life to be acceptable to the highest sticklers, but I do not despair that *someone* will have you."

He bowed his head meekly, saying, "Thank you. Do you have anyone in mind?"

"No, that is up to you."

"Your generosity overwhelms me. Unfortunately, I cannot think of any suitable lady it would amuse me to marry."

"I talk not of amusement, Marcus. I am speaking of marriage."

"I fear that I should make the devil of a husband, ma'am," he said apologetically. A thought crossed his mind, and he looked questioningly at his aunt. "By the by, does Kendle know of this?"

"Not yet. It is none of his business. He will get this house when I die, and of course he has his father's fortune. My own estates come from my mother — she never liked Kendle, you know, and would be only too pleased to know that the fortune was going to a Helston."

"Even such a one as I, ma'am? That is a risk, surely."

"I have known you all your life, Marcus, and I am sure that you would not waste your time and money at the gaming-tables if you had other responsibilities."

Sir Marcus smiled slightly. "Again I thank you; your faith in me is truly astonishing."

"You are aware of my conditions — I want to see you established."

"I am not sure that I am ready to be leg-shackled," he objected mildly.

"You are six and thirty, which is certainly old enough!" came the acid retort. "Now, do not keep me waiting, boy! I want your answer!"

The gentleman produced from his pocket an enamelled snuffbox and helped himself to a delicate pinch.

"I will consider it, your Grace. More than that I cannot say."

The Dowager settled back in her chair, a faint smile on her austere countenance.

"Then I must be satisfied with that for the present. With my backing you can make a very creditable alliance."

She picked up a small bell resting on a table at her elbow, and its shrill summons brought an aged footman to the salon, bearing a tray.

"A glass of port to seal our bargain, nephew?"

"Forgive me, your Grace, but I did not think we had yet made one."

"That you will consider the matter will suffice. I shall alter my will as I please, but I warn you, Marcus, you must mend your ways or you shall not touch one penny!"

He raised his glass to her.

"As you wish, ma'am."

"And do not think to pull the wool over my eyes," she warned him sharply. "I am very well informed of the events in Town."

"Evidently," replied her nephew drily. He studied his glass for a moment. "Perhaps, your Grace, you know something of the Tremayne family?"

"I remember old Percy Tremayne; he died some years back."

"It is his daughter that interests me."

"Cynthia — Lady Carfax." The Dowager shot a suspicious glance at him. "I did not think married ladies of that sort were quite in your line, Marcus."

"They are not. I refer to Lady Rosalyn."

"Is she in Town then? I knew she had returned from Belgium with Farradae's party, but I thought she would remain in the country."

"Lady Rosalyn inherited the Frencham property, and has recently moved into Brook Street. Quite a piece of perfection, too."

The Dowager gave a crack of laughter.

"You have little chance there, my boy! The Tremaynes are far too high in the instep for you."

"Indeed? My dear aunt, you interest me."

"They are related to some of the best families in the land, and the old Earl left both his daughters with a considerable independence. Lady Rosalyn does not need to go looking for a husband, especially if the Frencham fortune is as large as they say."

"But with your not inconsiderable settlement, am I not to be considered?" asked Sir Marcus lightly.

"A girl who could bring Carfax up to scratch in one season is unlikely to be interested in such a one as yourself!" came the sharp reply.

Sir Marcus was unabashed by his relative's opinion of his character, but continued, "Forgive me, ma'am, but you go too fast. I thought we were speaking of Lady Rosalyn Tremayne."

"We are." She saw the puzzled look on his face. "Come Marcus, surely you remember?"

"I fear not. I have a shocking memory, you know," he apologised, but she was not attending.

"But of course! It was at least ten years ago, and you were at sea then, were you not?"

"I believe I was serving aboard one of His Majesty's frigates. I pray you will enlighten me."

"Well, following her presentation, Lady Rosalyn was an overnight success, and at the end of a brilliant season she was engaged to young Carfax, then the biggest prize on the Marriage Mart. Everyone was agreed it was a splendid match — I remember they made a very handsome couple."

"Go on, ma'am."

"The Tremaynes left Town for the summer, and Carfax went with them. Nothing more was heard until the winter, when a notice appeared in the *Gazette*. Lady Rosalyn had terminated the engagement. When Carfax came back to London in the spring, he refused to talk about the matter. The younger Tremayne girl, Cynthia, was presented the following season, and shortly after that she became Lady Carfax."

"And Lady Rosalyn?"

"She was not seen for years. Her

mother died soon after her first season, and I believe she remained at Dowrings with her father until his death. That was about five years ago. After that she accompanied her aunt, Lady Farradae, to the Continent."

"And no-one knows the reason she cried off?"

The Dowager shook her head.

"Of course there was a great deal of speculation, and it was said her father was furious about it — refused to allow her out of the house, but I do not know if that is true. Rosalyn was always a very spirited girl, and it is most likely that she quarrelled with Carfax and cried off."

"It is possible she stood aside for her sister," he mused. "Lady Rosalyn is still unmarried."

"Possible, but unlikely. Cynthia was still in the schoolroom when Rosalyn was presented — and Tremayne was a stickler, he would never allow a child of his to socialise before she was presented. It was generally believed at the time that Carfax, having set his mind on marrying a Tremayne, took second choice — it is not without precedent."

"And what will the wagging tongues make of the jilt's return, I wonder?" Sir Marcus rolled the stem of his wine-glass between his long fingers, studying the crystal as though an answer could be read in its intricate pattern.

The Dowager shrugged, losing interest in the conversation.

"I would prefer you to turn your mind to your own affairs, Marcus."

He rose, laughing softly.

"I promise you I will. But surely, Kendle should be told before you alter your will?"

"I have told you it is no concern of his what I do with my private monies!"

She held out her hand. Sir Marcus took it and bowed low over it.

"I doubt if he would agree with you."

The old lady's thin hand clung to

his own for an instant.

"It would mean a great deal to me, Marcus, to see you settled," she said urgently.

His eyes softened fractionally, and he looked a little amused.

"I fear that the ladies you have in mind would prove dull company, and those that would amuse *me* would fall far short of your approval," he murmured.

The drive back to Town afforded Sir Marcus time to reflect on his situation. The Dowager was very near the truth when she spoke of his deep play. He had suffered serious losses, certainly. He smiled to himself: how the devil she knew about the little lovebird under his protection he did not know, but there at least he would be able to please his aunt. Clara was beginning to bore him with her tantrums and constant demands for trinkets — expensive tastes, too. He must certainly end that liaison, and soon. He made a mental review of his present finances. He was indeed at low ebb for the present, but he was an optimist — his luck at cards should change soon, and if not, there was always marriage. He preferred to dally with the dashing young matrons who were looking for a little excitement — like young Lady Murchiston, who had been throwing out lures to him for some time, now. His mind went over the alternatives to marriage: there was only one real option open to him, to sell Helston — the estate had been mortgaged in his father's time, and the Hall and its immediate park were all that was left unencumbered. He was not fool enough to delude himself that his fortune could be recouped by burying himself at Helston. Soon after his father's death he had realised that the estates had been milked dry and a great deal of investment would be needed to bring them back to their former prosperity. The task had proved too daunting for a young man, and he had instead gone to sea, hopeful of a fabulous prize money with which to restore the family fortunes. There had indeed been some financial gains, but nothing like the vast sums needed for the task, and Sir Marcus, disillusioned, had made his home in London, closing his mind to the problems of his estate.

However, he was no fool, and was honest enough to admit that the situation could not be ignored much longer. The Dowager had offered him an option: a respectable marriage, backed by her own wealth, which was certainly sufficient to recover some of the mortgages and set in motion a programme of improvements — it was his one chance to keep Helston. In his heart Sir Marcus knew there was no real choice, he would do what he could to save his birthplace.

5

TRUE to her word Lady Rosalyn was making a point of being seen with her sister. Her pleasure in such occasions was not unmixed, for although they could talk easily enough when Carfax was absent, if ever he joined the party Rosalyn was aware of a tension in the air. It was therefore with some reluctance that she accepted Cynthia's invitation to join a party at the theatre. She was even less enthusiastic when she learned who else was to be present: Rosalyn was shopping in Bond Street with her sister when Cynthia spoke of the forthcoming event.

"I have invited an old friend of yours to join us tomorrow, Ros," she said, as they settled themselves comfortably into the carriage, having completed their purchases.

Lady Rosalyn looked up enquiringly.

"It is Mr. Stayne — he tells me you were frequently in company together on the Continent."

"Richard Stayne?" Lady Rosalyn was surprised. "I would not call him a friend. An acquaintance, merely."

"You do not like him?" asked Cynthia. "For my part I find him very amusing."

"Oh he is, in a shallow sort of way." Rosalyn glanced curiously at her sister. "He told you we were friends? You must take care not to let him impose on you, Cindy."

Lady Carfax laughed. "You are too severe, Ros! I find him amusing, no more."

Rosalyn had to be satisfied. She knew Mr. Stayne to be a man of ready address, and a general favourite of the ladies, but she had never been more than distantly acquainted with him. Perhaps Cindy hoped to promote a romance, and to protect Carfax, thought Rosalyn wryly.

In the event it was not Mr. Stayne's presence at the theatre that unsettled her, as she recalled the following day, when Mrs. Windhurst came down to breakfast eager to discuss the play.

"You were so quiet when we drove home, dearest, that I knew you were too tired to talk then. I thought it quite excellent, did you not? Lady Macbeth looked so sinister, too. I vow she frightened me. Did you enjoy it, Ros?"

"Very much," replied Rosalyn, spreading a thin layer of butter on her bread. "I thought the performance very spirited. It was for just such entertainments that I returned to London, and I intend to repeat it as often as I am able. But not," she added thoughtfully, "in Damien's party."

Mrs. Windhurst glanced up sharply, but she could detect no emotion in her cousin's face. After a pause, she spoke, although she seemed to have difficulty finding the right words.

"Does it give you pain to see him,

101

Ros? Perhaps — perhaps it is too sharp a reminder of the past."

The green eyes flew up to meet Mrs. Windhurst's questioning glance, but only for a moment, then they were veiled again.

"If it were only my own emotions, I would not worry so," she said carefully.

Mrs. Windhurst nodded. "I too have noticed the distinguished attention that Carfax is wont to pay you. But he is devoted to Cynthia, surely he would not jeopardise that — "

Rosalyn put out her hand in a little helpless gesture.

"Of course he loves her! But I think at present he does not know it. God knows, I do not wish to come between them."

There was silence while both ladies considered the situation. Mrs. Windhurst looked up once as if to speak, but changed her mind. After a while, she tried again, choosing her words carefully.

"I fear that — your single status

makes you very vulnerable, Rosalyn. An eligible alliance must surely preclude Damien's attentions — " She trailed off, flushing slightly.

Rosalyn sat motionless, her attention fixed on her plate. After a moment she looked up and fixed her clear steady gaze on her cousin.

"I will not marry without love, Amelia. You of all people should know that."

"I should not have spoken," replied Mrs. Windhurst contritely, "forgive me."

Lady Rosalyn smiled. "It matters not, love. To be truthful, the same thought had crossed my mind, but that is not my object in coming to Town." She laughed suddenly. "I can see that if I wish everyone to believe that, then I must copy old Miss Nettleton, wandering about with a shawl continually dragging behind me, and being rude to everyone I meet!"

"That eccentric! Oh, Rosalyn, she must be fifty at least!"

"Am I to understand by that remark that I must wait until I attain that age before you will believe I am happy to remain single? What can I do to convince the world that I am serious, Amelia? Perhaps I should begin by cultivating an outlandish appearance — what think you, cousin?"

But Mrs. Windhurst was not to be drawn by her cousin's jokes, and she told Rosalyn that she was going out before she could be teased any more.

There was nothing eccentric in my lady's apparel when she attended the Tyndrum's ball a few days later, and she looked to be in the best of spirits. However, when she saw her sister arrive alone, she was aware of conflicting emotions: relief for herself that she need not be on her guard against his attentions, and dismay for her sister. Cynthia was in high good humour, thought Rosalyn. Too high, for her laughter had a brittle quality that she could not like, but a crowded ballroom was no place to invite confidences, and

Rosalyn tried to put the matter out of her mind, at least for the evening.

She noticed Sir Marcus Helston entering the room, and stiffened: their eyes met for an instant, and he inclined his head in recognition. Lady Rosalyn's icy stare and barely perceptible nod seemed to amuse him, but he did not approach her. Before the evening was half over, Rosalyn felt boredom creeping upon her. Somehow, she could find little to amuse her in the idle gossip of the ladies, and her dancing partners seemed more than usually dull. She caught sight of Cynthia dancing with a young gentleman in a canary-yellow waistcoat, who was obviously besotted by his partner. Rosalyn stifled a sigh, wishing she had not come. She moved to one side of the room, wondering if Amelia would object if she made her excuses to leave early.

"A very dull evening, is it not, Lady Rosalyn?"

She started, looking round quickly to find Sir Marcus at her side.

"If you find us so dull, sir, I am surprised you remain here!" she retorted.

There was a decided twinkle in his eyes as he looked at her.

"Would it please you to know I remain only in the hope that you will dance with me?"

"Not in the least!" came the swift reply.

He was not noticeably dashed by this, and he made no attempt to move away. After a moment's silence, she stole a glance at him, piqued by his unconcern.

"You should know I have been warned against you, Rake Hellborn!" she informed him.

"Alas, you have found me out — I am suitably chastened, and must now do what I can to redeem myself in your eyes," he replied gravely.

"You are not in the least chastened, and you are certainly past redemption!" she returned, trying not to laugh.

"My aunt does not think so, I assure

you. Let me tell you about her!"

"I cannot see what your aunt has to do with it."

"Quite a lot, as a matter of fact." He looked towards the centre of the room. "They are forming a set for the next dance — will you join me?"

Sir Marcus held out his hand to her. Rosalyn hesitated; she had been determined to keep him at a distance, and she was not at all sure that she liked his abrupt manners. Rosalyn looked at him, undecided. He met her eyes, a coaxing smile in his own.

"Come," he urged her softly.

Rosalyn shrugged inwardly, and put her hand in his. After all what harm could one dance do?

Sir Marcus made a good partner, and since he made no attempt to flirt with her she soon relaxed and began to enjoy herself. She even allowed him to persuade her to stand up for the next dance, and after that made no demur when he led her away in search of refreshments. With practised ease he located two empty chairs, and procured two glasses of champagne.

"Tell me, Lady Rosalyn," he began as he took his seat beside her, "do you know my aunt, the Dowager Duchess of Kendle?"

She frowned a little. "No, I think not. She must be important to you, sir, since you have mentioned her twice already this evening."

"She is. She has promised to leave me her fortune, if I fulfil one condition."

"Oh? And what is that?"

"That I make a respectable marriage. I thought you might like to consider it."

Rosalyn was sipping her champagne, but at his words she choked. She looked up at him incredulously.

"Do — do you think your aunt would approve of me?" she enquired, her lips quivering with laughter.

"Oh, undoubtedly. You are rich, very beautiful — a trifle high-spirited perhaps, but no serious defects," he replied solemnly.

Rosalyn laughed.

"You are abominable!"

"What, because I wish to marry you? Unjust, ma'am!"

"Am I to understand you are seriously making me an offer?" gasped the lady rather startled.

"Well, that was my intention — but perhaps I have been a little hasty."

"Much too hasty! I would not dream of such a thing!"

"Oh. Never?" he asked her hopefully.

Lady Rosalyn fought back her laughter.

"Never, Sir Marcus," she said firmly. "I wish you will stop talking in such a silly fashion!"

He sighed audibly.

"Perhaps you can put me in the way of some other respectable female who might help me?" he commented.

Her lips quivered, and she said, "You are incorrigible, sir, and I will not listen to you a moment longer!" She rose. "I see my cousin over there and I will join her immediately."

Sir Marcus, rising also, caught her hand and raised it to his lips.

"And, will you, nill you, I will marry you!" he quoted softly.

Rosalyn flushed, pulling her hand away.

"I am no Kate for you!" she flashed, and moved away into the crowd.

Amelia Windhurst was standing on the far side of the room, and as Lady Rosalyn joined her she said quietly,

"Oh, my dear, was there ever such a dull evening? So few of our particular friends here, and a host of encroaching mushrooms! I thought better of Jayne Tyndrum — she must positively *enjoy* being flattered and cajoled by these toadies! I wonder why we ever came — Cynthia has already left, complaining of the headache."

Rosalyn noticed with a shock that the dancing had ended and that people were beginning to leave. Their carriage was ordered, and while she waited for it to arrive at the door, Lady Rosalyn realised that she had spent best part of the evening with Sir Marcus, and when, in the privacy of their carriage, Mrs. Windhurst felt it her duty to point out to Lady Rosalyn the impropriety of spending the evening in the pocket of such a man, she could only hang her head and listen in silence. The worst of it was that she had not realised how time had sped by — a mischievous little smile curved her mouth in the darkness: it was shocking, but she had to admit to herself that she had enjoyed his company — except his silly talk of marriage, of course. He had brightened up a dull night for her. But it would not do to inform Amelia of this.

Lady Carfax, leaving the ball some hours earlier, travelled home alone in her coach, feeling tired and dejected. Carfax had been right, it had proved to be a most boring evening, but since she had decided she wanted to attend, he could at least have escorted her there, instead of taking himself off to his club in such a disagreeable manner! It had proved to be a most miserable evening, for Cynthia had missed his company. She thought bitterly that Rosalyn had not appeared to notice anything amiss — she had spent most of her time with Sir Marcus Helston, standing up with him for two dances, and they had been sitting with their heads together when she had left. A pity Damien had not been there to watch, she thought spitefully. The carriage pulled up outside Carfax House, and Cynthia went straight up to her room. She had thrown off her cloak and was sitting before her mirror when there was a knock on the door. Carfax entered.

Cynthia dismissed her maid, who was waiting to help her to undress, and she then turned her attention to the mirror, unclasping the beautiful sapphire necklace.

"I trust you enjoyed yourself tonight."

"Oh, of course!" replied my lady. She glanced at his reflection in her mirror. "Did you go out?"

"No."

He stared down at her cloak for a long moment, then walked over and put his hands on her shoulders, his eyes meeting hers in the glass.

"Did you miss me, Cindy?"

Lady Carfax gave a tinkling little laugh. "Miss you? Lord, no," she replied airily: "it is not in vogue for a husband and wife to live in each other's pockets."

She paused, hoping he would contradict her, but he remained silent, moving away from her. Her spirits sank a little at his lack of response. "Rosalyn was there," she said, watching him carefully. "She seems very great with Rake Hellborn."

Carfax looked up, a frown on his face.

"You had best warn her of that fellow — he is dangerous."

Cynthia tittered angrily.

"Warn Ros? Not I! She would not thank me for meddling in her affairs!"

"A word of warning, no more. She

is your sister, and deserves that much," he replied gravely. "Perhaps Amelia will mention it."

Cynthia closed the lid of her jewel-box with a snap.

"Oh, do stop talking of Rosalyn! If you are so concerned for her, perhaps *you* should speak to her."

In the mirror she watched as his mouth tightened, and he turned away, heading for the door.

"Damien!" Lady Carfax flew from her stool to place her dainty form before him. She smiled a little, putting her hands upon his shoulders. "Oh, Damien, let us not quarrel — it is so stupid. I am sorry," she said penitently.

His face relaxed, and he smiled at her. "I, too, am sorry. Let us forget the matter. How would you like me to arrange a quiet little dinner-party for us tomorrow night?" he suggested.

"Oh — Carfax, I am already promised to attend a soirée at Wotton House. Perhaps another night?"

He removed his hands from her

waist, disappointment written on his face.

"Yes, perhaps. Goodnight, my dear."

He bestowed a light kiss on her cheek and was gone. Lady Carfax rang for her maid to help her into bed, feeling very low indeed.

The following morning was bright and sunny, and Cynthia rose early, determined to show her husband a cheerful face and perhaps even to persuade him to accompany her on her shopping trip. When she arrived downstairs, she was disappointed: Lord Carfax had already left the house, and had left no message for her. She made a poor breakfast, and returned to her room to change her morning-dress for a warm walking-dress in deep blue, with a matching pelisse. A new poke bonnet in blue silk helped to restore her spirits, and she set out for Bond Street in an open carriage, feeling much happier. It was a bright, sunny day, and when she had completed her shopping Cynthia decided to call in upon her sister before returning home. She instructed the coachman accordingly, and was admitted to Brook Street as Mrs. Windhurst emerged from her bedchamber.

"Is that you, Cynthia?" she cried from the top of the stairs. "Come up, my dear. You will not object if I have a little breakfast while you are here? I overslept this morning, you see."

"Of course you must carry on with your breakfast, Amelia. Am I too early for you?" Lady Carfax followed the widow into the breakfast-room.

"No, no, my love. We stayed very late at the Tyndrum's last night — my dear, was there ever such a dull set! I swear I was ready to leave by midnight. How wise of you to go early, Cynthia! I do not know how Ros manages to be up with the dawn each morning! I was still at my chocolate this morning when my abigail informed me that Lady Rosalyn had already left the house — riding with Carfax! I wish I had half of her energy. No doubt you wish to wait for their return?"

Lady Carfax paled; her hands tightened in her lap as she struggled to collect her wits.

"No — I was on my way home and thought perhaps they — they may have returned, but it is of no consequence — I shall see Carfax later."

Cynthia rose. "I will not stay, Amelia. There are matters I must attend to. Pray, do not get up — finish your breakfast. You must not stand upon ceremony with me!" She smiled bravely, and took her leave.

Mrs. Windhurst continued to satisfy her hunger, blissfully unaware that her visitor had left in a very distressed state of mind: hurt, dismay and anger warred within her. When Lady Rosalyn returned an hour later, however, Amelia was immediately aware that something was wrong. Rosalyn burst into the drawing-room, where Amelia was engaged in knotting a fringe, and one glance at her stormy face was enough to inform her cousin that all was not well. She laid aside her work and waited expectantly. Lady Rosalyn looked down at her accusingly.

"Did you tell Damien that I — that I allowed Sir Marcus to *monopolise* me last night?"

"Goodness no!" replied the widow, surprised. "I was still asleep when you left the house this morning — I have not seen Carfax."

"Of course! I am sorry." Rosalyn flung herself down into a chair, her eyes smouldering. She jerked the kid riding-gloves roughly between her hands.

"He had the effrontery to tell me that I would ruin my chances of ever making a good alliance if I spent too much time with men like Rake Hellborn!" she announced, an angry flush on her cheeks.

"No doubt he is only thinking of you, love," replied her cousin mildly.

"Oh, I doubt it not! But I am old enough to handle my own life! Cindy must have informed him! I vow I thought she had more sense than to try to run my life."

Mrs. Windhurst glanced at the angry face, with the glittering green eyes and lips compressed into a thin line, before replying with unusual candour,

"Since you always run counter to her advice, perhaps she wishes you to make a disastrous match!"

There was a moment's silence, then Rosalyn laughed, her face clearing.

"Oh, Amelia! How right you are! But in this case I do not mean to be contrary — I have no intention of encouraging Sir Marcus. I have already made my own decision on that!"

"If that is the case, I suggest you forget the matter. Cynthia called a little earlier, and no doubt she is waiting to hear how Damien fared."

"Is she? Well, if Carfax repeats only half of the things I said to him, Cindy will know I will brook no interference in my affairs!"

Unfortunately, when Carfax returned home, he was greeted with the news that his lady had the headache and did not intend to leave her room that day. With Lady Rosalyn's tirade still ringing in his ears, he shut himself away in his library, wrathfully consigning all women to the devil.

6

LADY ROSALYN might not appreciate her brother-in-law's advice, but his words remained stubbornly in her mind. She was not in the least afraid of losing her heart to Rake Hellborn, but she was fully alive to the censure she would incur from society if she encouraged his attentions; Damien had angered her by his interference, but it had been the elemental truth in his criticism that rankled. She was unused to censure; her Aunt Farradae had been an easy-going chaperone, and under her aegis Lady Rosalyn had enjoyed more licence than was commonly granted to unmarried ladies. She had never passed the bounds of propriety (she thought somewhat bitterly that her only indiscretion had been to disobey her father and cry off from a very advantageous alliance with the very wealthy Lord Carfax), but she was now in danger of being thought fast if she should continue a friendship with a self-confessed fortune-hunter, and although she might shrug off the slightly cool reception she had received from a few of the elderly matrons of her acquaintance, she could not ignore the hints of such good-natured well-wishers as Lady Beezley that she should 'spread her favours a little more widely, to avoid being thought particular in any *one* direction'.

The advice of her friends came to Lady Rosalyn's mind as she was travelling to a literary soirée at Sedgefield House a few days later, and she resolved to behave with the utmost propriety, and give no-one cause for alarm on her behalf. Rosalyn and Amelia were amongst the first to arrive, and they chose to sit at the side of the room, where they hoped to avoid the crush. Mrs. Windhurst arranged her skirts becomingly around her on the elegant sofa, and settled back with a sigh.

"There! We shall be most comfortable here, I think, for we are unlikely to be crowded when everyone goes through to the supper-room, nor will we be roasted by that blazing fire that Julia Sedgefield has had lighted."

"And we will be able to slip away without fuss should the evening become too dull to endure," remarked Lady Rosalyn, her eyes twinkling.

"Nonsense! I am sure we shall be enchanted. Mr. Urville is to read his new poem, 'Ode to a Song Thrush', and Mrs. Consett will recite from Shakespeare."

"What is that to one who remembers the great Mrs. Siddons?" declared Rosalyn grandly. She smiled. "Do not worry, Amelia. I shall try not to disgrace you by yawning too openly, although from what I have seen of Mrs. Consett these past few weeks she finds far more enjoyment in her recitals than her audience ever does!" Lady Rosalyn looked about her with interest.

"The room is beginning to fill, now. I see Lady Beezley's party has arrived, and the Greenows are present, too. Is that the Murchistons over there, Amelia? Good God! Major Franklyn — and that must be his mama! I told you when we accepted this invitation it could prove intolerably dull, now I am sure of it. Do look at her grey gown, Amelia! One would think she was as poor as a church mouse, dressing in such a way."

"My love, you are a very severe critic tonight. To be sure, the lady's apparel is a little — sober, but perfectly suitable for a widow."

"Yes, very dull and respectable," replied Lady Rosalyn cheerfully. "I have no doubt Carfax would approve of an alliance there!"

Amelia laughed. "I would not wager on your chances of happiness, however, the Major is far too staid to enjoy your more outrageous tricks!" A sudden suspicion crossed her mind, and she eyed Lady Rosalyn warily. "I trust you are not planning a misalliance, to annoy Carfax?"

"Goodness, no! I may be angry at Damien for trying to dictate to me, I know there is some truth in his arguments. Heavens! I see Sir Marcus has arrived. I should not have thought this was at all his sort of thing. Now, Amelia, you will see just how well I will behave. You notice I give him but the slightest nod of the head, and he does not dare to approach. Instead he takes himself off to the card-room, so you may now be easy! How wise of Mrs. Sedgefield to set aside a haven for those among us who do not share her literary tastes."

"You may joke me, Rosalyn, but for my part I hope that dreadful man will remain in there all evening, and leave us in peace!"

Mrs. Windhurst's hopes were not to be realised. Mr. Urville's ode having been read, and politely applauded, and various other short works recited, there was a break in the proceedings.

Mrs. Windhurst moved away from her cousin to speak to Lady Greenow. She had exchanged no more than a dozen words with that lady when she saw Sir Marcus approach Lady Rosalyn and sit down beside her. She was dismayed, but short of returning and ordering Sir Marcus to leave (which he would very likely refuse to do, she thought bitterly), she was powerless to prevent his conversation with Rosalyn, and could only hope that her cousin would dismiss him quickly. Lady Rosalyn did indeed greet the gentleman coolly, but he was not noticeably abashed, and took his seat beside her without invitation.

"Did I not see you in the Park with Lady Carfax yesterday?"

Lady Rosalyn inclined her head.

"My sister was kind enough to take me up, yes. I usually ride a hired horse in the mornings, but my hack cast a shoe, and I decided upon a walk in the Park."

"Lady Carfax is a notable whip, I

believe, and I understand your father the late Earl was considered something of an expert."

"Yes. He taught my sister to handle the ribbons. I think she does him credit."

"And yourself?"

"I never learned the art," she replied simply.

"I would have thought that Lord Tremayne would have taught you both," remarked her companion casually.

"My father and I were not — close."

"A pity. I have no doubt you would have made an apt pupil."

"Thank you. I should like to learn, I think."

Sir Marcus helped himself to a pinch of snuff from an elegant enamel box.

"That is easily remedied — let me teach you."

"You are very kind, sir, but I could not impose upon you."

Lady Rosalyn could not but be flattered, for Sir Marcus's ability to handle a team was well known, but she knew she must decline.

"It is no imposition: you would pick it up in no time, I am sure."

"I am honoured, Sir Marcus, but I think not."

"Why?"

"You must see that it would not be at all the thing for you to teach me to drive," replied Lady Rosalyn, flustered.

"No, I don't see." His eyes glinted down at her. "What I *do* see is that you consider it improper to accompany me in an open carriage, with a groom sitting up behind us. What possible harm can I do to you in that situation?" he demanded.

Lady Rosalyn suppressed a smile.

"You are a notorious rake and a self-confessed fortune-hunter, and it would not enhance my reputation to be seen with you," she replied primly, while her eyes danced with mischief.

"Baggage! No, don't fire up. I will not press you further. Tell me instead what you think of the literary offerings you have heard tonight."

She wrinkled her nose, searching for the right words.

"They are very — emotional, some of them. Very dramatic. But I am no expert of course," she replied guardedly.

"You think them pretty poor stuff, do you? Then we are agreed on that point! There is an excess of words and sensibility this evening."

"Since you have been in the card-room all evening, I do not see how you can pass any opinion."

Sir Marcus smiled.

"How gratifying that you should take such an interest in me," he murmured wickedly.

Lady Rosalyn flushed slightly, but decided it would be wise to ignore this remark. Instead, she said stiffly,

"I wonder you should be here, sir, if you are not entertained."

"Oh, I am well enough amused, ma'am," he replied, and she followed his glance towards the centre of the room, where Lady Murchiston was standing, smiling and nodding at Sir Marcus in what Lady Rosalyn considered to be a most unbecoming way.

"It would appear your presence is required elsewhere," she observed drily.

"But say the word, Lady Rosalyn, and I shall remain here for the remainder of the evening."

"Well, I do not wish to stay here!" she retorted, with a laugh. "My cousin returns, you see, and you must vacate her seat!"

"As you wish," he sighed audibly.

Sir Marcus rose as Mrs. Windhurst approached, and with a slight bow to the ladies he sauntered off towards Lady Murchiston.

Amelia's disapproval showed plainly on her face, and Rosalyn could only be grateful when another aspiring poet stood up to speak, and silence was called for. There were no further opportunities for speech until supper was announced, and the two ladies rose thankfully from their seats.

"At last! I thought that young man would never stop," declared Mrs. Windhurst in a low voice. She shook out her skirts, hoping aloud that the creases would soon disappear. When she looked up, she found Major Franklyn had appeared with an invitation from mama that they should go down to supper together. Ignoring Rosalyn's beseeching look, Mrs. Windhurst smiled kindly at the Major.

"Unfortunately, I am already engaged to join Lady Greenow, but I am sure she will not object if Rosalyn stays with you." She patted Rosalyn's hand. "Off you go and enjoy yourself, love, and I shall be with you again after supper."

Mrs. Windhurst moved away before Rosalyn could reply, satisfied that she was in respectable, if rather dull, company. After that there was nothing for Rosalyn to do but to place her fingers on the Major's arm, and go with him to the supper-room.

"Mama has gone with Mrs. Berrett — her companion, you know, an excellent woman — so we may expect to find that they have secured for us a comfortable table with no draughts to trouble us. Ah! There they are, in the corner."

As they drew near, Rosalyn perceived how alike were mother and son. Mrs. Franklyn was a plump woman, with a sallow, unhealthy complexion. With her pale, protuberant eyes and wide, drooping mouth, she reminded Rosalyn of a bullfrog, and the impression was enhanced by her sagging chins, which were imperfectly supported by the ruff on her dress.

The introductions were made, and Mrs. Franklyn turned her baleful stare towards Lady Rosalyn.

"Thomas has told me a great deal about you, Lady Rosalyn."

There was nothing encouraging in Mrs. Franklyn's tone, but Rosalyn smiled cheerfully as she took the soft, plump hand that was held out to her.

"And he has told *me* a great deal about yourself, ma'am. I know he has a high regard for you."

"Flavia and I were discussing the merits of the poetry we have heard, were we not?"

Mrs. Franklyn turned towards the small, bird-like lady beside her, who replied with a wide smile, "Indeed we were, Mrs. Franklyn, and exceedingly touching I have found some of it. How I envy such talent, to be able to write such affecting lines."

"For myself," replied Mrs. Franklyn heavily, "I find the tone of tonight's offerings to be beyond what is generally pleasing — there is a want of delicacy, of modesty, in the passions that are described. It puts one to blush."

The idea of such a regal personage as Mrs. Franklyn blushing caused Ros to smile inwardly, but she turned her attention to Mrs. Berrett, who was replying in her twittering little voice.

"I understand these stanzas are

very tame compared to Lord Byron's works."

"Then I am glad he has gone abroad, for I cannot think his writings appropriate for a lady's drawingroom."

"Come, come, Mama," put in Major Franklyn, in a jovial voice, "Lord Byron is accredited one of our finest poets, by all the young ladies, at the least." He turned to Lady Rosalyn. "No doubt you too are a slave to his genius?"

"I enjoy reading his works, certainly, but I am not mad about them," replied Lady Rosalyn coolly.

As supper progressed, she began to realise that the Major had inherited his pompous attitude from his mother, a very opinionated woman. Hardly touching her food, Mrs. Franklyn favoured Rosalyn with her ideas on a number of subjects, and in between she fired a series of questions at her guest, concerning mainly her background and her inheritance. Such conduct did not endear her to Lady Rosalyn, who considered it an impertinence, but she discovered that Mrs. Franklyn was as impervious to snubs as her son, and she could only hope that she might soon find an excuse to take her leave. She bore very little part in the ensuing conversations, leaving the bird-like Mrs. Berrett to reply to Mrs. Franklyn, which she did in a fluttery, nervous way. Rosalyn felt a little sorry for her, supposing that she was dependent upon Mrs. Franklyn, and thus compelled to agree with that lady. Rosalyn found her attention wandering, until it was suddenly recaptured when the Major mentioned a name she knew.

"I had understood, Mama, that this evening was to be solely devoted to literary readings. That is the reason I was so desirous that you should attend. Imagine my chagrin, therefore, when I arrive to find that our hostess had set aside a card-room — it was bound to encourage quite another element to be present, the young bloods who care nothing for art, only for gambling. The foremost amongst them, of course, is

Sir Marcus Helston."

"I do not doubt that Mrs. Sedgefield acted with the best intentions, but I wonder she should allow that man into her house." Mrs. Franklyn leaned forward a little in her chair, her chins trembling with indignation.

"I understand he has wasted all his fortune, and he has not two pennies to rub together, but what he can win at cards."

"But his birth is impeccable, ma'am. There are many with less right to be here," put in Rosalyn, a spark of anger in her eyes.

"Undoubtedly, but one cannot always allow birth to be a mark of what is acceptable in the world, and in Sir Marcus's case I find there is a sad want of propriety that cannot please."

"Do you, Mrs. Franklyn? Personally, I find him very amusing," replied Lady Rosalyn, irritated by the older woman's assumption of authority.

Mrs. Franklyn eyed her disapprovingly, and even the Major looked a little disturbed by this frank admission.

"I understand he is a desperate flirt," tittered Mrs. Berrett.

"For my part I have always found him most courteous," returned Lady Rosalyn, conveniently forgetting her previous encounters with Rake Hellborn. "In fact, I merely mentioned that I have never learned to drive and he immediately offered his services."

Major Franklyn smiled condescendingly. "What impudence!" he said in a comfortable tone. "You must know, dear Lady Rosalyn, that should you wish to learn to drive, I am completely at your disposal."

"What a pity I did not know it earlier," said Rosalyn, affably, "for I have now accepted Sir Marcus's kind offer."

"Did I hear my name? Your servant, ma'am. Lady Rosalyn. Evening, Franklyn."

Sir Marcus had strolled up behind them, and Lady Rosalyn turned to bestow a brilliant smile upon him.

"You did, sir! I was telling Major Franklyn how you had kindly offered to teach me to drive."

Accepting this reversal without any visible sign of surprise, Sir Marcus bowed.

"You are honouring *me*, ma'am, by accepting my poor services." He smiled at the assembled company before turning his mocking glance towards Lady Rosalyn once more. "I have come to take you back to Mrs. Windhurst, if you are ready, my lady. She has been looking for you."

"Of course. If you will excuse me, Mrs. Franklyn, I must return to my cousin."

Lady Rosalyn bestowed her glittering smile upon the Major, and walked off with Sir Marcus.

"Am I to understand that I have the dull Major to thank for this change of heart?" he enquired when they were out of earshot.

"But of course! I am quite out of temper with him, and his mama!"

"Then shall we say tomorrow morning, ma'am, if you are free?"

"For what?"

"Your first driving lesson. Since you say you have changed your mind and decided to accept my offer, I naturally supposed that you would wish to start as soon as possible."

Lady Rosalyn hesitated. She knew that her cousin would strongly disapprove of her driving out with Sir Marcus, and her own reason told her that to be seen with the notorious Rake Hellborn could do her no good.

"Unless, ma'am, you feel you cannot face the gossip that would most certainly arise," he mocked gently.

Rosalyn rose to the bait.

"Fustian!" she retorted. "Tomorrow morning will suit me admirably."

In the following weeks, Lady Rosalyn's behaviour was such that it drew protests from her closest friends, but to no avail. She met Sir Marcus on the friendliest of terms, and could be seen driving with him every day. She even went so far as to dance twice with him one evening at Almacks, a club Sir Marcus rarely attended. Rosalyn did not explain her actions to anyone, even her cousin, who remonstrated with her most strongly.

Town life was proving to be all Rosalyn had hoped for, but her pleasure in it was not unmixed. Her recent inheritance had made her a very wealthy woman, and she was well aware that to this fact she owed the attentions of more than one gentleman. At least Sir Marcus had been open with her about his intentions, and she found it easy to relax in his company. There was another reason for not discouraging him, but this she hardly admitted to herself.

She had known from the start that her return to Town would stir up old memories, and she was already aware of gossip concerning herself and Lord Carfax. Whatever her own feelings might be, she was sure he did not truly love her, although at present his sentiments might be a little confused. She had no intention of giving the scandal-mongers reason to believe there was anything more than friendship between them, and in this respect the appearance of Sir Marcus in her life had been well-timed, for he had drawn all eyes away from Damien, and Rosalyn hoped that her brother-in-law's ill-concealed infatuation for her would quickly burn itself out. Thus she was deaf to Mrs. Windhurst's protests, and although she made sure he did not live in her pocket, Sir Marcus was fast becoming one of her most frequent visitors at Brook Street.

Lady Rosalyn soon mastered the art of driving, and she lost no time in setting up her own stable, with the help of Williams, her father's groom: a letter to her cousin at Dowrings, asking him to spare her this old family retainer, had been promptly answered by the appearance of the servant himself, who had informed my lady that the Earl was more than happy to let him go, since he was selling most of the horses.

Rosalyn was shocked.

"What! All of them?"

"Most of 'em, my lady. Half the stable was closed up soon after the new lord took over, and there's very little use for those that's left. The Earl does not hunt, and it's better that they shouldn't be left eating their heads off in the stables."

Williams had known Lady Rosalyn since she had been a baby, and he was well aware of the meaning of the sparkle in her eyes.

"The old lord would not have wished his hunters to be wasted, my lady. He always held that they enjoyed the chase as much as he did," he said meaningfully.

Rosalyn's stormy green eyes met his steady gaze, and he thought at first she had not understood him, then the colour returned to her cheeks, and she looked away.

"Yes, of course. My father was not

sentimental about his horses, was he? Caroline must be costing Harvey dear if he must sell them all," she added to herself.

She felt as if another link with her past had been severed, for the stables had been her joy at Dowrings: they might disagree on most subjects, but the fifth Earl and his daughter had been at one in their love of hunting, and Rosalyn's happiest memories of her father concerned the chase.

She dragged her mind back to the present, and ten minutes later Williams left the house with a clear idea of his lady's requirements, while Rosalyn waited for Sir Marcus, who was to take her driving in the Park that afternoon. The news from Dowrings had unsettled her, and Sir Marcus found his companion unusually silent. They entered the Park gates and had travelled some distance when he broke the silence by asking, in his abrupt way,

"I wish you would tell me, Lady

Rosalyn, why you continue to drive out with me."

"Oh — because I enjoy it — you amuse me."

"Thank you." He looked down at her enigmatically. "You have said no more than a dozen words since I took you up today, which does *not* amuse me!"

Rosalyn flushed guiltily.

"Forgive me — I was thinking of — other things."

"Your sister, perhaps?"

"Partly, yes."

"Are you worried about that fellow Stayne who is hanging around her? Oh, do not look so startled, my dear. Everyone knows he is uncommonly attentive to her."

"I confess I cannot like it — I do not trust that man, he has a most unsavoury reputation."

Sir Marcus gave a crack of laughter.

"The same could be said of myself, ma'am," he reminded her.

"No, that is a different matter. You

have always been honest with me."

"Which is more than you have been with *me*." He heard her sharp intake of breath, and glanced down to meet her surprised gaze. "You think that by encouraging my attentions you are pulling the wool over society's eyes, where you and Carfax are concerned. No, don't deny it — in general no doubt you are succeeding admirably, but you are *not* hoaxing me."

Rosalyn looked down at her hands, clasped tightly in her lap.

"You are very frank!"

"I like to think so."

She drew a breath and said slowly, "There is nothing between Lord Carfax and myself, Sir Marcus, but you are probably aware that we were betrothed, a long time ago?"

"I had heard that, yes. What happened?" he asked conversationally.

There was a pause before Rosalyn replied in a low voice.

"He — I decided we should not suit. My return to London has rekindled old memories, you see, and I know that people are watching, to see if — if they can uncover an intrigue between us!" she ended bitterly.

"And you prefer that they should link your name with a dubious character like myself? Very commendable."

His tone was dry, and Rosalyn hung her head.

"I am sorry," she said, searching in her reticule for her handkerchief. "Perhaps you had best take me home."

"If that is your wish."

"I never meant to use you," she said presently, in a small voice.

"I am happy to have been of service," he replied politely.

"At least you cannot accuse me of raising false hopes. I have always made it quite clear that your suit was hopeless," she continued, with some of her usual spirit.

"Indeed you have, ma'am. Which reminds me, I would like to take you to meet my dear aunt next Thursday. I think you would like her."

"The Dowager Duchess of Kendle?" She looked up at him suspiciously. "If you mean to press your suit with me, Sir Marcus — "

He laughed.

"No, I assure you, nothing like that. Although if my aunt approves of you, I cannot guarantee not to resume my efforts in that direction."

Rosalyn looked up to find him laughing at her, his eyes alight with amusement, and she could not prevent herself from smiling back at him. He held her eyes for a moment.

"Will you come?" he asked her quietly.

"Yes — no — you have not told me why I should," was the somewhat flustered reply.

"You would like her. She is an old lady of great spirit, and although her age keeps her out of Town, she seems to know more of what is going forward there than anyone else of my acquaintance." He saw the indecision on her face, and continued, "I will call for you at ten o'clock on Thursday morning. Can you be ready at such an early hour?"

"Of course! But I have not yet agreed to go with you."

Sir Marcus was guiding his team out of the Park, and he gave his attention to negotiating the city traffic before replying.

"Since you have used me so abominably over the past weeks, I think it is the least you can do, as some small recompense."

Lady Rosalyn bit her lip, torn between amusement and remorse. The curricle turned into Brook Street, and Sir Marcus brought his horses to a stand at her door.

"Well, ma'am, am I to have the pleasure of your company?" he asked as he helped her to alight, adding by way of persuasion, "I have no doubt your dear friend the Major would advise you most strongly against it."

"How abominable of you to use such arguments on me!" She laughed at him. "Very well! I will go with you, but only so that I may tell the Dowager exactly what I think of her scapegrace nephew!"

"Then you will find her in complete agreement with you." He lifted her hand to his lips. "Until Thursday, then, my lady!"

7

"YOU were very late last night." Carfax turned his attention from the generous helping of ham before him, waiting for his wife's reply. Lady Carfax did not look up from her own breakfast.

"I was at the Dunnets' — everyone stayed late."

"I take it Stayne was your escort?" My lord spoke with studied indifference, but Lady Carfax looked at him suspiciously.

"He was, but what of it? I told you I wished to go, but you would not take me," she responded petulantly.

"I merely requested that we stay home — is it too much to ask, to spend an evening with one's wife?"

Cynthia flushed a little. "No doubt if Rosalyn had been attending you would have shown more interest."

Carfax set down his fork with a clatter. "Oh my God! How can you say such things? Must I tell you over and over again there is nothing between Rosalyn and me — I am married to you!"

His harsh tone brought the tears to her eyes, but Cynthia would not let them fall.

"No doubt you wish you were not!" she flashed.

"When you act this way, madam, yes!" he retorted, losing his temper.

Immediately he was sorry, but before he could speak again a servant entered to clear the table.

Lady Carfax surreptitiously wiped her eyes. At length the footman withdrew, and she rose, holding her dainty head proudly. "If you will excuse me, my lord," she said in icy accents, "I have an engagement this morning."

Carfax rose, stretching out his hand across the table towards her "Cynthia, I — "

But my lady was gone.

Lady Carfax might not resemble her sister in looks, but both ladies possessed the stubborn pride that had characterised their father, and it now came to Cynthia's aid. She felt her world falling apart; Damien's remarks proved he did not love her, but for all that she would not cry. She forced herself to take special care over her appearance, and when she left the house an hour later, only her closest friends would have noticed anything amiss in her demeanour.

She spent over an hour with the fashionable modiste who enjoyed her patronage, displaying a spurious interest in the latest materials and styles that were displayed before her. She felt loath to return to Carfax House, and after commissioning two very expensive gowns from Madame Sophie, she set out to do a little more shopping. The purchase of three charming (and costly) bonnets did much to restore the balance of her mind, but even the addition of a pair of lavender kid gloves, a new reticule and a pair of exquisite satin dancing-slippers did not completely dispel her depression, and she returned home with a severe migraine, which laid her low for the remainder of the day.

After a solitary dinner, Carfax went up to his wife's apartments, but upon being informed by my lady's personal maid that her ladyship was quite knocked up, and not wishful to see anyone, he took himself off to Brooks's.

"Ah, Carfax, just the man! Come and join us!" cried one portly gentleman, engaged at a card-table.

"Aye, come and sit in, Damien. Alex is out already, and Helston here has the devil's own luck," commented a young man in a cherry-red waistcoat, moving his chair to make room for the newcomer. Lord Carfax looked across the table at Sir Marcus, sitting back at his ease, with a pile of rouleaus on a small table at his elbow. Sir Marcus smiled a little, and did not fail to note the faint look of dislike on Damien's face.

"My luck appears to be in tonight, Carfax. Do you care to challenge it?" he drawled.

Carfax shook his head. "Thank you, no. I do not gamble tonight."

The man in the red waistcoat laughed. "Damien is the only one I know who can come to Brooks and *not* gamble."

Sir Marcus, keeping his eyes fixed on his cards, murmured provocatively, "How dull."

Carfax flushed, but said nothing.

"You are off to Belfort soon, are you not, Carfax?" asked another gentleman.

"In a couple of weeks, Hugh. Do you care to come?"

That gentleman shook his head. "I am off to visit m'father — best to keep on good terms with the old fellow, you know — my allowance depends upon't."

"Try telling that to Marcus," called another voice.

The gentleman named Hugh looked across the table with interest. "What's this, Helston?"

Sir Marcus merely smiled, but the portly gentleman looked up to explain: "My wife had it from the Duchess of Kendle that the Dowager — Helston's aunt, you know — has willed her fortune to him, so long as he makes a respectable marriage. Kendle's furious, of course."

Carfax, his attention caught, hovered by the players. Someone laughed.

"I would give a monkey to see Rake Hellborn leg-shackled!"

There was general amusement at this, and Sir Marcus cast a swift glance at Carfax before replying, "I am considering the idea, however. Now, shall we continue our game?"

The following night, Lord Carfax escorted his lady to a masquerade ball. He tried several times to open a conversation, but each attempt was met with such an icy response that he eventually abandoned the effort. They entered the ballroom, already hot and crowded, and he made good his escape, leaving his wife to enjoy her sulks. If it caused him any pain to watch his wife change from a small iceberg into a gay and laughing young woman, he did not show it. Cynthia watched her husband from the corner of her eye, and saw him make his way around the room, a smile here, a word there, until he was lost in the crowd. Well, she thought angrily, if he does not care, then so do not I! Her own fixed smile became brighter, and she danced and chatted to her partner as though she had not a care in the world.

Later that evening, Lady Carfax observed Damien talking to Rosalyn and Amelia, and she made her way towards them, holding out her hands to her cousin, and kissing her sister affectionately. However jealous she might be, pride would not allow anyone to guess at it.

"I have been telling Rosalyn and Amelia, my dear, that we shall be delighted to have them at Belfort next month," said Carfax.

Cynthia felt a coldness within her. She had always intended to invite Rosalyn to Belfort, but to her over-sensitive mind the fact that Damien had already issued the invitation seemed but more proof of his regard for Rosalyn. However, she stifled such feelings and smiled brightly.

"We would love to see you both there. Please say you will come!"

"You must know I shall be delighted, Cindy, but I cannot speak for Amelia."

Mrs. Windhurst shook her head. "Unfortunately, I must decline. I have been away from my own house long enough. It is time I returned to attend to all the little matters that I have neglected."

"But you will come back to Town, will you not?" asked Lady Carfax.

"Oh, assuredly — if Ros will have me. I shall rejoin her here in the autumn."

"Should my sister be so uncharitable

as to refuse to house you, you must stay with us!" cried Cynthia playfully. She caught sight of Sir Marcus approaching, and turned to him, holding out her hand in an unusually friendly manner. "Ah, Sir Marcus! The very person I wished to see! Carfax and I are gathering together a small party of friends to join us at Belfort this summer — nothing formal, you understand — we should be delighted to count you one of our number."

★ ★ ★

Helston raised his brows fractionally at this uncommonly warm reception. He bowed over her outstretched hand, replying, "Delighted, ma'am."

His eyes travelled from Lady Carfax to her husband, who was looking on disapprovingly, and an imp of mischief danced in his eyes as he accepted the invitation. His own particular devil prompted him to go further, and he

158

turned his attention to Lady Rosalyn.

"I trust you have not forgotten our engagement tomorrow, my lady?"

"By no means — I look forward to it," said Rosalyn.

She saw Damien's jaw tighten, and she tried to make light of the matter by an explanation.

"Sir Marcus is taking me to meet the Dowager Duchess of Kendle, Cynthia: she knew Mama, I believe."

"Perhaps you would care to join us, Lady Carfax?" murmured Helston, helping himself to a delicate pinch of snuff.

Rosalyn froze, her eyes fixed on Carfax as she prayed he would not rise to the provocation that Sir Marcus was so obviously throwing at him. Cynthia, conscious of the tension in the air, hastily declined, and looked appealingly at her sister.

"I trust you will not be late tomorrow," put in Rosalyn before anyone else could speak. "I believe you said ten o'clock, did you not? Now, if you will excuse me, I see an old friend of mine that I would like to make known to you, Cynthia." Rosalyn turned to her cousin, who was standing silently beside her. "Amelia, you had best come too — I am sure you will remember Mrs. Pooley."

The ladies moved away, and Sir Marcus was alone for a moment with Lord Carfax.

"No doubt you would prefer me to absent myself from your gathering. Shall I make my apologies and stay away from Belfort?"

"My wife is at liberty to invite whom she pleases," Carfax replied shortly, before walking away.

When Sir Marcus called for Rosalyn promptly at the appointed hour the following morning, he found her ready and waiting for him, but his compliments on her punctuality were received with only a distant nod. He gave her a speculative glance, but said nothing more until they had passed through the busier thoroughfares of the Town.

"I trust you are warm enough, Lady Rosalyn?"

"Perfectly."

"Then perhaps you would care to loan me the travelling-rug that is wrapped around you, for I feel distinctly chilled this morning."

She did not pretend to misunderstand him.

"You deserve to be. You were abominable last night!"

"I confess I was thrown a little when your charming sister invited me to join her party."

"You should have refused."

"Why?"

"Because — oh, you know very well why!"

"No, I don't — tell me," he returned cordially. "There's no need to worry about my tiger — soul of discretion, I promise you!" he said, as she glanced back at the groom, sitting up behind them.

Rosalyn drew a breath, searching for her words.

"My sister issued the invitation to you to make Carfax angry, I think," she told him.

"And perhaps to offer him a rival for your affections?"

"That's absurd! If Cindy were not such a little fool she would see that Carfax cares only for her — his concern for me is purely fraternal."

"Then there is no reason at all why I should not make one of your merry crowd," he argued reasonably.

Lady Rosalyn turned her head away. "You are not very amusing, sir."

Recognising the hurt in her voice, he took one of her gloved hands in his own strong grasp. Rosalyn felt the power in his fingers, and she was conscious of a strong desire to cling to his hand, but resisted the temptation.

"I am sorry," he said. "I did in fact offer to pull out, but Carfax told me his wife could invite anyone she wished." Helston looked down at her. "I will stay away, if that is what you really want."

Rosalyn hesitated, twisting her hands together in her lap. "I — shall not be sorry to see you at Belfort, Sir Marcus."

Having assured himself on this point, her escort set out to restore their former easy friendship. Since he could be very charming when it pleased him, this was easily done, and they were soon in perfect accord. The miles sped by, and after a while Rosalyn lapsed into silence. Sir Marcus, glancing down at her, saw a thoughtful look on her face.

"You seem serious, my dear. May I share your problem?"

Rosalyn started out of her reverie, a mischievous twinkle appearing briefly in her eyes.

"No problem, exactly. Since they concern you, though, I do not think I should tell you my thoughts."

"That is unfair! Of course I should know what concerns me!"

"Well, it is a constant source of amazement to me," she said thoughtfully, "that no matter what — excesses — a man may commit, as long as he is rich and well-born, he is still considered an eligible parti, while a gentleman like yourself, whose pockets are to let, is constantly referred to as a libertine, a notorious and dangerous rake."

"But if we were to be married, my sweet, I would then be a very rich man, and my 'excesses', as you call them, would be of little account," he replied.

"There is no question of our marriage, sir, but *if* such an unlikely event were to take place I should insist that your excesses stop immediately!" she retorted swiftly.

"What, all of them?"

"All of them!" she said severely, biting her lip to hold back the laughter bubbling up within her.

Sir Marcus shook his head sadly, saying, "What a boring life we should lead."

This was too much for Rosalyn, who burst into laughter.

"Odious man! I beg you will not say another word on the subject, it is most improper!"

"As you wish, ma'am."

Soon the horses slowed to a trot, and they turned off the main road and into the short wooded drive leading to the Dowager's house.

They came to a stand before the massive oak doors of the house, and Sir Marcus jumped down from the curricle and walked round to help Lady Rosalyn to alight.

A liveried servant appeared at the door, led them through the marbled hallway to the stairs, and up to the Dowager's apartments on the first floor. The room was oppressively hot, for, despite the sunshine pouring in through the widows, a fire blazed in the hearth. The Dowager Duchess was seated close to the fire, her back to the light, making it difficult for Rosalyn to see her features. As the servant closed the door, leaving the Dowager alone with her guests, she spoke in her abrupt manner.

165

"So you have brought her, Marcus. Well, my dear, come forward and let me look at you! Hmm, you have your mother's eyes, but otherwise I should not take you to be her daughter."

"She was very beautiful, was she not?" remarked Rosalyn, unperturbed. She moved forward to touch the thin, beringed fingers that were held out to her. "I believe my sister resembles her more closely," she added.

The Dowager, pleased with Lady Rosalyn's calm response to her direct attack, allowed herself a small smile.

"Sit down, my dear. Not there — here, where I can see you. Marcus, you will find a decanter and glasses over there, bring Lady Rosalyn a glass of wine, and one for me."

Sir Marcus obeyed this peremptory command silently, and when he handed Rosalyn her glass she saw a smile in his eyes.

"Perhaps I should tell you immediately, your Grace, that I have not the slightest intention of marrying your nephew."

The old lady gave a cackle of mirth. "Ha! A woman of spirit!"

"Common sense, merely. Sir Marcus is a care-for-nobody, with a very dubious past," returned Rosalyn bluntly.

"You hear that, Marcus? Well, my dear, I cannot say in truth that I blame you for not wishing to ally yourself to such a scoundrel, but if that is the case, why did you allow him to bring you here?"

"Sir Marcus has talked of you a great deal, and I was curious to meet you," said Rosalyn frankly.

"How wise of you not to wish to marry my nephew — you are obviously a very sensible young woman," decided the Dowager, sipping her wine.

Sir Marcus was moved to protest at such treachery within his family, but the Dowager shook her head at him.

"I warned you how it would be, Marcus, if you continued your rake-hell ways! I doubt if you will find any sensible woman to have you."

"But I do not wish to marry *any*

sensible woman, ma'am," he replied, his eyes resting on Lady Rosalyn.

Rosalyn met his gaze squarely for a fleeting moment, then she lowered her eyes, veiling her thoughts from him. The interchange was not lost on their hostess, but she said nothing, merely smiling to herself.

"Your Grace has a fine park here at Duffley," commented Lady Rosalyn, rising from her chair and going to the window, "a most charming prospect."

"It has always been a favourite of mine. The park was planned by my grandfather — your great-grandfather, Marcus — it formed part of the settlement when I married the late Duke. It will pass to my son when I die — although I feel sure Kendle would like to have it now if I would but move to the Dower House."

Sir Marcus took out his snuff-box and tapped the lid thoughtfully.

"But does this estate not belong to Kendle? I thought everything had passed to him."

"It does, but he is too afraid to ask me to get out!"

Rosalyn smiled, and glancing across the room at Sir Marcus she found he shared her amusement.

"I understand Mr. Frencham had several estates, Lady Rosalyn," the Dowager continued. "Do you intend to keep them all?"

Rosalyn shook her head.

"I am selling most of the property. I shall keep the London house, of course, and one of the small estates in Hertfordshire. I understand it needs a little attention, but I feel sure it will prove adequate for my plans."

"May one enquire the nature of these — ah — plans?" put in Sir Marcus idly.

"I intend to set up my own establishment there — with a suitable female companion, of course," she said, somewhat defiantly.

"You seem very sure of yourself — have you no thoughts of matrimony?" asked the Duchess in her forthright manner.

"None, your Grace."

"A most unusual young woman." The Dowager flicked her sharp eyes to her nephew. "I'll tell you to your head, Marcus, that you are a fool if you do not make a push to engage this lady — she's a woman of substance, a rare quality these days!"

"Pray, ma'am, do not put me to the blush," cried Rosalyn, a laugh trembling in her voice.

"Indeed I do know it." Sir Marcus shook his head sorrowfully. "But I have given my word to the lady not to speak to her of marriage, lest I forfeit the pleasure of her company ever more."

Sir Marcus, noticing the first hint of tiredness in his aunt, brought the interview to a close shortly after, and Rosalyn was surprised to see from the long-case clock in the corner that they had been with the Dowager for over an hour. The old lady held out her hand to Lady Rosalyn, remarking in her blunt way that she was welcome to call at Duffley whenever she chose, should she ever find herself passing that way. Rosalyn murmured her thanks for this honour, and accompanied Sir Marcus out of the house.

"Well, what do you think of my aunt?" Sir Marcus put the question to his companion as they made their way back to Town.

"You were correct in assuming I would like her — she is a most entertaining lady."

"I am glad you think that, and I know my aunt enjoyed your company. Unfortunately, most of her visitors present themselves as a matter of duty, and since they are usually too frightened of her to make any but the most inane utterances, the Dowager finds them very dull."

"How sad! But my impression is — forgive me if I am mistaken — that she positively enjoys terrifying her guests."

"She did not frighten you, however," said Sir Marcus with a smile.

Lady Rosalyn turned her head towards

him, saying, "You are very fond of the Dowager Duchess, are you not?"

"She is the only member of my family who does not preach propriety to me. She also bailed me out a few times when I was younger, and had outrun my allowance."

"But surely — your father — " Rosalyn broke off, flushing.

"My father took no interest in my affairs, especially my gaming debts. What I did not know then was that he could not have paid them anyway. He had already lost most of his fortune the same way. Are you beginning to pity me? There is no need: I have made little attempt to repair the family fortunes."

Rosalyn could think of no suitable reply to this, and when, after a brief pause, her companion produced some unexceptional topic of conversation, she gladly followed his lead.

When they reached the city, Rosalyn was aware of a vague sense of disappointment that the journey was almost over, for she had enjoyed herself far more than she had thought to do.

"Do you care to drive out with me tomorrow morning, ma'am?" asked Sir Marcus, helping her to alight.

"No — that is, I would like to drive *you* around the Park, if you have the nerve for it," said Rosalyn, her green eyes twinkling. "Williams has set up my stable for me, and he acquired a curricle and pair of match bays for me only yesterday, which I have yet to try out. You need not be alarmed, Williams assures me the bays will give me no trouble. Perhaps you have seen them — they are from Marriner's stable."

"I heard he was selling up some of his livestock. It surprises me, Lady Rosalyn, that you settle for a mere curricle — I had thought you would wish for a phaeton and four at the least," he quizzed her.

"Crane-necked, no doubt!" laughed Rosalyn. "I do not aspire to those heights. At least, I wish to gain a little more experience first! Well, sir, will you allow me to take you up?"

Sir Marcus bowed.

"Certainly. I have sufficient confidence in my pupil for that."

He climbed back into his own vehicle, giving her a mocking salute with his whip as he set off, and she watched him disappear around the corner of the street before going inside.

8

SUMMER approached. Town grew warm and uncomfortable and the Ton moved away to fashionable watering-places or their country estates to while away the summer months. Lord and Lady Carfax departed from Town a little earlier than most, my lady being desirous to see her children, and to oversee arrangements for the accommodation of their guests, who were to follow later. Carfax and his lady had been distantly polite to each other for some time, and Damien hoped that once at Belfort, without the continuous round of balls, routs and parties to distract them, they might regain their former happiness, but it was not so simple. Cynthia, detecting no sign of the lover in her kind, courteous husband, devoted herself to the children. Carfax accepted the rebuff with resignation, and threw himself into the affairs of his estates, which needed attention.

Lady Rosalyn was the first of the guests to arrive at Belfort. She travelled north with her maid, and as the well-sprung coach bowled along she looked forward to the visit with mixed feelings. She had not been to Belfort since Cynthia had been mistress there, but despite her long absence the road was uncannily familiar.

"We will catch our first glimpse of the house when we reach the top of this hill," she said aloud, but although she awaited the sight eagerly, the shock of her emotions when Belfort appeared below made her tremble. The house was set in the centre of a large park, where sheep, cattle and deer grazed peacefully together. It was a square house, built of stone and standing white in its verdant setting. Gazing down upon it, Rosalyn recalled vividly the thrill of her first visit — she had been just eighteen, with her highly successful presentation behind her and the prospect of a very advantageous marriage to look forward to. It had seemed to her that she was fortune's darling, having everything her heart desired.

How short-lived that happiness had been! First the sorrow of her mother's lingering illness, through which Rosalyn had so patiently nursed her. Carfax had remained at Dowrings for much of the time, unwilling to leave lest he should carry with him some infection. She had had very little time to spare for him, and her father, anxious and powerless to help his beloved wife, rarely left his room to attend to his guest. Into this disordered household came Cynthia, returning from the select seminary that had tried to instil in her the accomplishments necessary for a young noblewoman.

With the benefit of hindsight, Rosalyn thought it was inevitable that her beautiful young sister, freed from the strict surveillance of her teachers and left to her own devices, should tumble headlong into love with Carfax. She wondered when he had known of his own change of heart. Rosalyn set her mind to remember that painful time, trying to recall any look or word that should have warned her, but it was useless. She tried to recall his face when, shortly after the death of her mama, Carfax had taken his leave, promising to return soon: she could remember that moment — surely he had loved her then! Rosalyn had fallen ill herself shortly after, and what followed was lost to her. They told her she had been close to death, but she could remember nothing until that fateful morning when she had felt well enough to leave her bed — Rosalyn could see it so clearly, the sun streaming into her room, her desire to enjoy a little fresh air after weeks spent lying in her bed. She had decided not to call her maid, but to open the window herself, to prove how much better she felt. Her room was in the west wing of the house, overlooking the shrubbery, and as she gazed out she could not fail to see Cynthia and Carfax, deep in conversation and exchanging such looks of love that she could not mistake —

The road swept on across the hill, allowing travellers a prolonged view of the house before it plunged down into the dark woodlands that bounded the park. The coach barely checked at the lodge gates, and moments later they were at the house. Rosalyn found Lady Carfax awaiting her in the Great Hall. She thought her sister's greeting a little strained, and when Cynthia had shown her to the apartments set aside for her, she begged Cindy to stay.

"We have seen so little of each other that I should like to talk, if you are not too busy?"

"If you would like me to stay, then of course I am only too happy to oblige you," replied Lady Carfax formally.

Rosalyn ignored the cool tone. She removed her hat, and surveyed her hair in the looking-glass.

179

"How flat my curls have become! I find bonnets a sad trial, do not you? Jane spent a great deal of time arranging my hair this morning, only to have it crushed!" Rosalyn glanced up at her sister. "Your hair always looks so beautiful, Cindy! I see you have taken to wearing a cap, my love. Very fetching; what does Carfax think of it?"

Cynthia looked away, her fingers toying with the ribbons on her gown.

"He has not said — I do not think he has noticed."

"Abominable man!" cried Rosalyn in a rallying tone. "You must *make* him notice, love! You should walk to and fro before him until he cannot fail to see you!"

Rosalyn paused, carefully watching her sister's reflection in the glass. A small sob from Cynthia brought Rosalyn to her side in an instant. She put her arms around Cynthia and hugged her.

"There, there, my pet."

Instinctively, Rosalyn uttered the words she had often used when they were young, and now she felt Cynthia relax against her.

"Oh, Ros! It is useless! He does not love me," sobbed Lady Carfax.

"But of course he does, love. I am convinced of it."

Rosalyn held her sister away from her and said slowly, "I can promise you one thing, my dear. There is nothing between Damien and myself, if that thought has worried you."

Cynthia wiped her eyes, saying in a trembling voice, "You may say so, Ros, but you cannot persuade me that Damien does not love you — the way he looks at you when you are together — "

"It is not so! Oh, I may have thrown him a little off balance when I returned to London, but I am sure he loves you as much as ever, and I certainly do not love *him*."

"Do you not?" Cynthia looked at her sister wonderingly.

Rosalyn had uttered the words unthinkingly, but after a moment's pause for reflection, she smiled.

"No," she said softly, "Damien does not hold my affections."

Cynthia caught Rosalyn's hands between her own dainty fingers.

"I am glad of that, at least," she said earnestly. "But Ros, Carfax has been so distant of late. In fact, he once said that he wished he had not married me!"

"Now, Cynthia, pray do not begin to weep again! I have no doubt that it was said in a moment of heat, was it not? Very well then, you must coax him out of the sullens, my love — it is not impossible."

"But that is not all," replied Cynthia in a whisper. "He is very angry with me for inviting — someone here."

"Sir Marcus?"

Lady Carfax put her handkerchief to her lips and shook her head. "Mr. Stayne."

"Oh no, Cindy! Whatever possessed you to do such a thing?"

"Carfax ripped up at me for inviting Sir Marcus, and it put me in *such* a temper. I told him I should invite anyone I pleased, and so — so when Mr. Stayne came up to me later I invited him to join us. Not that I care what Damien says," she ended defensively, "I think Mr. Stayne is a most agreeable gentleman, and he is the only one who has shown me any kindness these past weeks!"

Rosalyn looked doubtful, but remained silent. The two ladies remained wrapped in their own thoughts for a time, then Rosalyn spoke.

"Who else has been invited to stay?"

"Apart from Sir Marcus and Mr. Stayne, there are the Greenows and the Penallys — you do not know them, I think. Mr. Penally is a cousin of Carfax. They have a son, Reginald, who is up at Oxford, and two daughters of marriageable age. I must confess that I do not always find myself in harmony with their mama — she always seems to have a better way of doing things, if you know what I mean. It makes one feel quite inferior at times! And she has a great deal of sense, but I never feel easy in her company — it is as if she were always looking for points to criticise."

"I think I understand you," said Rosalyn, nodding. "You cannot laugh at her for being foolish, and you feel guilty that you cannot like her."

"Exactly. I find it curious, though, that Penelope and Diana are so different! I have yet to find any sense in them at all. Their conversation for the most part concerns themselves, and fashion is their only interest. Of course, I have not seen them for some months, and they may have improved a little by now," added Cynthia charitably.

"Well, at least the numbers are balanced. We must hope that these young ladies will keep our single gentlemen amused."

Cynthia gave a chuckle.

"Unless they have changed out of all recognition, think they can be relied upon to do their best. They were always very forward girls."

"On the catch for husbands, are they?" Rosalyn's eyes twinkled with merriment. "How fortunate that we have two such eligible bachelors in the party!"

Cynthia laughed, but shook her head at her sister.

"Fie on you, Ros, how can you say so? I know of no objection to Mr. Stayne, but I am sure I shall incur Mrs. Penally's severe displeasure for allowing a person of Sir Marcus's reputation to come into contact with her children."

"Poor Cynthia! I do hope it will not persuade your cousin to cut short her visit."

"If it were to do that," replied Cynthia with a smile, "I should feel quite charitable towards Sir Marcus! I doubt it will make any difference — they never stay less than three weeks."

Rosalyn feared that her sister was once more sinking into a despondent frame of mind, and she changed the subject by enquiring after her nephews.

"I shall take you to meet them as soon as you are rested. John and little Charles are both anxious to see you. I have explained to them that you were in Brussels with the Duke of Wellington, and they now expect you to tell them about the fighting," warned Cynthia.

"Do they imagine then that I watched the whole?" said Rosalyn, amused.

"I tried to tell them that you were with the diplomatic staff, but I fear they misunderstood me," replied Cynthia with a chuckle.

"How dull they will think me, when I confess that I know little of the battles."

But Rosalyn was wrong. Within a few minutes of meeting her nephews, she was their favourite guest. She had taken the precaution of bringing a few gifts with her, including an ingenious mechanical toy drummer, which she hoped would amuse them, but more important was her ability to enter into their concerns. They soon lost their shyness before their aunt's warm smile, and when Carfax came into the morning-room shortly before dinner he found Cynthia and Lady Rosalyn enjoying a noisy game of lottery tickets with the children.

Rosalyn looked up with a smile. "I am hopelessly outclassed at this, Carfax, and must make my advanced years my excuse."

She rose, and gave him her hand.

"I am glad they are entertaining you so well. How are you, Lady Rosalyn?"

Lord John, a sturdy young man of eight summers, tugged vigorously at his father's sleeve.

"Papa, Aunt Rosalyn has promised to go riding with us tomorrow — if you do not object?"

"I see no reason why not, although I am surprised that Lady Rosalyn should wish to spend her time with such a pair of scapegraces." He smiled across at Rosalyn. "Do not let them bully you into accompanying them."

"I have no intention of letting them do so. In fact, I am assured the ride will be of great interest to me."

Charles, a year younger than his brother, but already as tall, tucked a small hand into Rosalyn's.

"You have told us you liked birds, Aunt Rosalyn," he said, "and John and I know where we can see *lots* of them; if you are not too tired, we will take you to see the nest we have found on the other side of the Home Farm."

Carfax laughed, and ruffled the boy's hair affectionately.

"I think there is little chance of your aunt being fatigued, unless it is from your incessant chatter."

"Mama says she is too busy, but perhaps you could come with us, Papa, to keep Aunt Rosalyn company," suggested Charles.

There was an uneasy silence. Carfax hesitated for a moment, then he said quietly, "I shall be very busy tomorrow. Perhaps another time. Now, I think

Nurse is waiting for you upstairs. Make your bows to the ladies, and off you go."

As the door closed behind the boys, Rosalyn turned to her sister. "If you think I could be of use to you tomorrow, Cindy, I can postpone my ride — "

"I could not countenance it, my love," smiled Cynthia; "John and Charles are so looking forward to it. Besides, I shall be pleased to have the children out of the house when our other guests arrive; boys can be so noisy. You see," explained Cynthia, "Mr. Gargeney, their tutor, is away for a few weeks, and they do not attend to Nurse as they should."

"Then I shall not feel guilty if I enjoy my ride with them, but instead think of it as a service to you!"

It was late afternoon when Lady Rosalyn and her charges returned from their excursion, and they were met with the news that Mr. and Mrs. Penally had arrived, and also Mr. Stayne. Lady Rosalyn looked down at her dusty riding-habit.

"We must all change before we meet them, I think. How long until dinner, Groves?"

The butler eyed the two distinctly dishevilled children.

"I shall order dinner to be put back an hour, my lady, and advise Lady Carfax of the delay," he replied woodenly.

Rosalyn's eyes twinkled. "We must hope that will be sufficient for us to make ourselves presentable. I trust there will be enough hot water."

Groves permitted himself the ghost of a smile.

"I have already arranged for it to be taken up for you, ma'am."

Lady Rosalyn came downstairs again a little less than an hour later, to find the other members of the party already assembled, including, she noted with some surprise, her two nephews. Their nurse must have moved swiftly to clean them up in such a short time, she thought.

"I am sorry to delay you, Cynthia. I hope you can forgive me," she said, her charming smile including everyone in its warmth.

"Of course, my dear," said Lady Carfax, rising from her seat.

"Mr. Stayne you know, of course, but let me introduce you to our cousins."

Mr. Penally was a pleasant-looking man, somewhat older than Lord Carfax and with a bluff good-humour that made him a popular guest. His wife was small, plump and self-assured: she was dressed neatly in a sober-hued gown, and her unremarkable brown hair was partly covered by a snowy lace cap.

When Rosalyn turned her attention from the parents to greet the Penally children, she was mildly surprised. In contrast to the former's neat apparel, the young ladies were dressed in the flimsiest of gowns, embellished with a great many ribbons and flounces.

Lady Rosalyn was aware that they were noting every detail of her own raiment, and she thought with amusement that they must consider her very dull, in her simple round dress of green silk, with a plain silk shawl across her arms. Her hair was caught up in a knot on top of her head, but although she wore no ornament save a string of pearls around her throat, the overall effect was one of elegance which left the young Misses Penally feeling vaguely overdressed. Mr. Reginald Penally suffered from no such uneasiness. He was sure that his canary-yellow waistcoat, dove-coloured small-clothes and sage-green coat could not but be admired. He made an elegant bow to Lady Rosalyn and paid her a few fulsome compliments which made her eyes dance with merriment. The young man then turned his attention to his father's conversation with their host, confident that he had made a very good impression with the lady.

By the time the party broke up

for the evening, Lady Rosalyn had formed a fairly accurate opinion of her fellow-guests, and the prospect of a protracted stay did not please her overmuch. Richard Stayne was apparently indifferent to his host's dislike, and seemed intent upon fixing his interest with Cynthia. Rosalyn was at a loss to understand her sister's behaviour: she seemed to be unable to repulse Mr. Stayne. Several times that evening he had addressed himself in a low voice to Cynthia, and she had blushed. Rosalyn was sure Carfax had also seen the incidents, and she felt certain he would not long countenance such behaviour under his own roof.

Then there were the Penally's. Lady Rosalyn had taken an instant liking to Mr. Penally, but found his wife to be a woman of decided opinions and very little humour. Of the three children, she thought Reginald foolish but harmless, and the two girls seemed incapable of holding a sensible conversation. Rosalyn admonished herself for being so difficult to please, and thought ruefully that the others were probably equally dissatisfied with her company. On this sobering thought she took herself to bed, hoping that the arrival of the remainder of the party would add a little more sparkle to the company.

By dinner-time the following day, the party was complete, with the Greenows and Sir Marcus arriving within an hour of each other, but as Lady Carfax took her seat at the dinner-table, she could only feel uneasy about the oddly assorted guests. Rosalyn might laugh at Diana and Penelope's attempts to gain the attentions of the gentlemen, but for her part she found their behaviour embarrassing. Mr. Stayne's presence was also disconcerting: she could not deny she was attracted to him, and her husband's coolness was thrown into strong relief by the other's close attentions.

The one hopeful note was struck by Sir Marcus, who was rapidly winning the approval of his host: Carfax was agreeably surprised in Helston, there was nothing in his manner to disgust, and his conversation was intelligent and entertaining. By the time the gentlemen quit the dining-room, Damien was fast reviewing his original opinion of his guest. In the drawing-room, Miss Penally was seated at the piano when the gentlemen entered, and her sister called across to her to remain.

"For I am sure," said Diana in a carrying voice, "that Papa would like to hear the new work you have been practising."

Miss Penally simpered and hesitated, but the polite encouragement of her hostess made her remain at her post, and she dashed through a Haydn Sonata with more gusto than accuracy. Sir Ingram Greenow moved across the room towards his wife, who was sitting beside Lady Rosalyn.

"Well, my love, how is it that you cannot meet Lady Rosalyn without you two must put your heads together?"

Lady Greenow laughed up at her

husband. "We are enjoying a cosy chat, Ingram. Pray do not disturb us."

"Lady Greenow has been giving me news of all my old friends — I have quite lost touch with so many of them since returning to England," explained Rosalyn.

"I fear you must delay your reminiscences," said Sir Ingram, looking over his shoulder, "Miss Penally has finished her recital and I believe our hostess is coming to persuade you to play for us, Lady Rosalyn."

"I am indeed," smiled Cynthia as she came up to them.

"Oh, but it is so long since I played — I am out of practice."

"Then we will make allowances for you," said her sister.

Rosalyn went to the pianoforte, and after running her fingers over the keys, she started to play a slow haunting tune. It was a simple traditional air, but it had been a favourite of her mother's, and Rosalyn found herself thinking back to that summer when her world had collapsed around her: within a few short weeks she had lost both her mother and her fiancé. As the last notes died away, she remained still, gazing into the past.

"A most sensitive performance, my lady."

Rosalyn started and looked up to find Sir Marcus watching her. She blushed and rose from the pianoforte.

"Will you not play again, Ros?" cried Cynthia in surprise.

She shook her head. "I am too much out of practice. And I have promised your sons that I would go up to the schoolroom to bid them goodnight, since they retired immediately after dinner."

With these words, she left the room, anxious for a few moments alone to collect herself. When she returned to the drawing-room, the candles had been lit, casting a warm glow over the assembled company. Card-tables were set up, and at one of these a game of whist was in progress with

Mrs. Penally and her son, and Lord and Lady Greenow. A much noisier game was taking place at another table, where Miss Penally and Mr. Stayne were paired against Miss Diana and her papa. Lady Carfax was engaged in sorting the silks from her work-box, and Rosalyn took a seat beside her.

"Poor Cindy, a houseful of guests and you are reduced to sorting silks."

"It is preferable to whist," came the low reply.

"What has happened to Damien and Sir Marcus? Have they deserted us?"

"They are playing at billiards," said Cynthia. "They seem to be enjoying each other's company."

"You sound surprised, but they are both sensible men. There is no reason why they should not get on. I know Sir Marcus can be very provoking," continued Rosalyn, seeing her sister's doubtful look, "but he can also be very agreeable, when it pleases him. I can assure you that he is certainly a favourite with the children. Soon after his arrival Sir Marcus was rivalling me as their favourite guest, and a chance remark that he had seen Lord Nelson in action gave him supremacy; he consolidated his position by telling them what I suspect were highly apocryphal tales of his days at sea!" she ended laughing.

"You like him very much, do you not?" remarked Cynthia in a casual tone.

"Why yes, I do. I was used to think him arrogant, and a care-for-nobody sort of person, a Rake Hellborn indeed! But he is both kind and considerate, to those he wishes to please."

Cynthia was alarmed at the soft glow in her sister's face — it was a look she had not seen there before.

"He has no fortune, Rosalyn," she said cautiously.

"Is that such a crime?" responded Rosalyn

"He is a self-confessed fortune-hunter — you told me so yourself!"

"Cindy, you goose, with my wealth

that would not matter!"

Rosalyn smiled at her sister's look of concern, and squeezed her hand affectionately.

"Pray do not worry yourself, Cindy, I enjoy Sir Marcus's company I admit, but that is all."

Lady Carfax was not convinced, but the entrance of a servant with the tea-tray at that point heralded the break-up of the card-parties, and she was obliged to turn her attention to her guests.

9

THE young Lord John and his brother quickly learned that their aunt Rosalyn was an early riser, and they would lie in wait for her as she made her way to the breakfast-room, in the hope that she could be persuaded to join in their games. Lady Carfax, leaving her room one morning at her customary hour of eleven o'clock, was appalled to learn that her sister had already spent a couple of hours with her nephews, playing at charades.

"You should not allow them to monopolise you, Ros. They have known you barely a week, and already they are taking advantage of your good nature," Cynthia admonished her.

Rosalyn only smiled, and shook her head.

"I do not allow them to 'monopolise'

me, as you put it, but I do enjoy their company. Besides, they tell me Mr. Gargeney returns tomorrow, and they will then have much less time to spare."

"That is true, but we did not invite you here to entertain the children, but that we might entertain you."

"But I *am* enjoying myself, greatly! Now, love, if you will excuse me, I see that the sun is now shining, and I am going to take a stroll in your beautiful rose garden before it begins to rain again."

Rosalyn delayed only to change her slippers for more suitable footwear and to fix a becoming straw hat over her curls, before making her way to the rose garden. It was a warm, sheltered spot, protected against the worst of the weather by high hedges on three sides, and the house on the fourth. The roses sparkled with droplets of rain, and Rosalyn moved slowly through the paths lined with bushes, enjoying their heady fragrance, and allowing her thoughts to wander. It was not long before she heard footsteps crunching on the gravel path somewhere behind her, and she turned to find Sir Marcus approaching. Rosalyn smiled.

"I would not guess you to be a lover of roses, Sir Marcus."

"In general I am not. I saw you from up there." He indicated the terrace which led off from the drawing-room and gave access to the rose garden by way of a grand flight of steps. "May I join you, ma'am?"

Lady Rosalyn showed her acquiescence with a slight inclination of the head, and they continued along the path in silence, pausing only for Lady Rosalyn to admire a particularly fine bloom.

"A splendid display of colour," commented Sir Marcus.

"My sister has made a vast improvement here; this was used to be a shrubbery, but the plants were old and past their best."

"You visited Belfort before your sister became Lady Carfax?"

There was a tiny pause before Rosalyn replied.

"I came here once or twice with Papa."

"And do your memories haunt your return?" he asked casually.

Rosalyn stopped to consider the point, her head tilted to one side.

"Strangely, no. I imagined I should be sensible of some agitation of the spirits when I first arrived here, but there was none — except a thankfulness that the journey was done," she added, trying for a lighter note. "By the by," she continued, "I understand my nephews have a great liking for you."

"I have promised to go fishing with them when the weather improves, as they assure me it will, very soon."

Rosalyn gave a gurgle of laughter.

"They are incorrigible scamps, but one cannot help liking them."

"If that is so, my dear, perhaps you would care to come with us," suggested Sir Marcus.

"Not I!" she retorted swiftly. "Perhaps

you should ask Miss Penally to accompany you." She stole a glance at him.

"But think of the children, ma'am. *You* would be their first choice. I'd not ask them to accept second best."

"No doubt Miss Penally's habit of addressing them as 'dear little boys' would not be to their taste," said Rosalyn, "but at least you would not need to fear that she would upset your excursion by contradicting you."

"Which is something you, madam, take delight in, I suspect!" he retorted. He glanced up at the clouds, which were gathering threateningly overhead. "We had best turn back — I believe a shower is imminent."

As he spoke, a raindrop splashed on a leaf beside him, and without ceremony he took Lady Rosalyn by the arm and hurried her back along the path towards the terrace. The storm broke as they reached the stone steps, and Sir Marcus grabbed his companion by the hand, almost pulling her up the steps, across the terrace and into the house through one of the drawing-room's long windows. He closed it behind them, and turned to face Lady Rosalyn, who had taken off her sodden hat and was shaking out her disordered curls.

"You have a raindrop on your cheek," he said, putting a hand up to her face.

She smiled up at him, a warm glow in her eyes.

"Ah, there you are, Lady Rosalyn! My dear, you are drenched! You must go upstairs and change before you catch a chill." Lady Greenow's admonition cut across the silence.

Sir Marcus let his hand fall, and Rosalyn, after one final brief smile, turned away.

"I am a little wet," she agreed, surveying her dripping gown. "I had best change immediately."

She left the room, smiling at Lady Greenow as she passed. That lady paused before following her, and looked thoughtfully at Sir Marcus.

"It was a little imprudent of Rosalyn to venture out in such conditions," she said slowly. "I do trust she will not suffer for it."

Sir Marcus returned her gaze steadily. "I am sure Lady Rosalyn knows what she is about."

The inclement weather continued, and Lady Carfax was kept busy arranging entertainments for her guests. She was glad to have an excuse to avoid Mr. Stayne, whose very marked attentions were beginning to disturb her. It was one thing to embark on a light flirtation with a guest, but quite another to allow it to develop into anything more serious under the very nose of one's husband. She therefore put him at a distance; she was too busy to ride out with him, too tired to take a walk, and when he asked her if he had in some way offended, she pleaded a headache. Richard Stayne realised he was pushing matters a little too fast, and changed his tactics. There was business to attend to in Town, he said. He had not intended to impose upon them for more than a few days, and already two weeks had passed. With practised ease Mr. Stayne took his leave and made his way to London, trusting that his absence would work to his advantage with Lady Carfax; she was a very beautiful woman, and he longed to possess her, but Mr. Stayne was a very practical man. He knew that he enjoyed the chase as much as the capture, and for this reason he steered clear of unmarried ladies, whose thoughts centred around catching a husband. He had had one or two narrow escapes from matrimony in the past, and he found the pursuit of married women a much more enjoyable pastime. The presence of a husband did not worry him unduly, since it added a touch of danger to the adventure, and in the event, very few husbands would risk the scandal of actually calling him out. In the present case he was sure that he had very nearly won Lady Carfax, all it needed was a slight nudge from Carfax and she would fall into his hands like a ripe plum! He was quite content to sit back and wait for a little while.

Mr. Stayne's departure may have relieved Cynthia of her most pressing anxiety, but it did not remove a tiny crease from her brow, which Lady Greenow noticed, and commented upon in her forthright way. The weather had cleared a little, and the two ladies were strolling together through the park which surrounded the house. It was unlikely that they would be overheard, and Cynthia felt free to confide in her friend.

"I am concerned over the growing intimacy between Rosalyn and Sir Marcus. No doubt you have noticed it?"

"My dear, I could not fail to do so! If Sir Marcus is in earnest, as he appears to be, then I wish them very happy."

"You approve the match?" asked Cynthia incredulously.

"His birth is respectable, and he can

be very amiable when he wishes to please."

"But he is a — a libertine, and a fortune-hunter! I cannot believe he will make Rosalyn happy."

"You should have considered that before you invited him to make one of your party," observed Lady Greenow drily.

Lady Carfax hung her head, saying in a small voice, "It was very wrong of me, I know it, and I shall never forgive myself!"

"Do not upset yourself, Cynthia. What is done cannot be undone, and for my part I think you should leave them to work out their own lives."

"But surely something *could* be done!" cried Lady Carfax.

"Do you wish to rob your sister of her happiness a second time? Oh yes." Lady Greenow nodded, seeing the other's startled look, "I have always known why Ros broke off her engagement in defiance of her papa."

"But — you have never spoken, never hinted — "

"It was not my business to interfere. Although when I think of the way the poor child suffered, with your mama gone, and Percy refusing to let her out of the house, I own I was tempted to speak my mind."

"I doubt if it would have helped. Poor Papa was so broken up when Mama died that I do not think he would listen to anyone. I was lucky that he let me come to London to live with my Godmother the following year — I was married from her house, you know. I was so happy to have Damien that I did not consider poor Ros, at home, bearing the full force of Papa's anger."

Lady Greenow considered her companion with a mixture of sympathy and contempt.

"I have known you both since you were born, Cynthia, and because of that I hope you will forgive me if I speak freely. Your sister sacrificed a great deal for your sake, and I think she is now entitled to her own happiness. Should she decide to marry Helston, I hope you will wish her good fortune, as I do — although I have no doubt others will disagree with me."

"Mrs. Penally has already spoken to me on the matter," commented Cynthia, keeping her eyes lowered.

"I trust you told her that it was none of her concern! No, I can see from your face that you did not!"

"The worst of it is that she has spoken to Damien, and told him he should step in." Cynthia's voice was hardly above a whisper.

Lady Greenow gave a sigh of exasperation, but replied hopefully, "Well, I have always thought Carfax a sensible man, and I am sure he will not interfere."

The improvement in the weather promised to continue, and Lady Carfax was insensibly cheered by this good omen. The younger members of the household pressed her to arrange an excursion for the following day, and after a lively discussion over dinner it was agreed that they should go to the nearby town of Milchester, which boasted a fine mediaeval church. Lord John and his brother were not overly enthusiastic about the plan, but when Carfax added that he would arrange for a cold collation to be prepared for them at the local hostelry they brightened perceptibly, and took themselves off to bed that night hoping for a fine day.

Their prayers were answered, and the party assembled after breakfast in high good humour. The Misses Penally had arrayed themselves in all their finery, with woollen pelisses sporting double shoulder capes and high poke bonnets trimmed with feathers and ribbons.

Lady Greenow, joining the others in the Great Hall, made her way to her husband, who greeted her jovially.

"Well m'dear — what's this? Are you going to drive out in that sober garb? You will be outshone, you know; our young ladies are set to take Milchester by storm!"

His lady smiled, replying in a low voice, "One cannot but wish that they would not wear *quite* so many ribbons and frills."

"If you want my idea of a well-dressed young woman, you have only to look at Lady Rosalyn over there — or her sister for that matter. Both dressed as neat as wax, yet they'll catch every man's eye for miles around, I'll be bound."

Lady Greenow felt compelled to frown at such a speech, but she was forced to admit that Rosalyn and her sister were both looking their best.

Sir Marcus complimented Rosalyn on her appearance as he handed her into the waiting landau.

"Thank you, sir. Your flattery over-whelms me."

"I do not flatter you — if I were to do that I should tell you you were the most beautiful lady present, but honesty compels me to say that your sister must take that honour."

"How cruel of you to cut me down so," said Rosalyn, smiling. "It must be a lesson to me to receive what compliments I can achieve with more gratitude!"

No more was said, for the rest of the party were taking their places. The carriages set off, with Cynthia accompanying Mrs. Penally and her daughters in one chaise, while Lady Greenow and Rosalyn were well entertained by their two young companions in the more cumbersome landau. The gentlemen rode some distance behind the carriages, with Mr. Penally regaling Sir Marcus with sporting anecdotes, and Carfax good-naturedly listening to Reginald's inconsequential chatter.

Milchester was reached without incident, and the carriages stopped at the gates of the church to allow the occupants to alight.

"The coaches will await us at the Pelican," explained Cynthia, smoothing her gown. "The men are riding on there now, and will walk back to join us, so we had best carry on without them."

She ushered her party into the grounds of the church and up to the main doors, pointing out the finer points of the building as she went. By the time the gentlemen arrived, they had entered the building and were duly admiring the fan-vaulted roof, stone panelling and excellent carvings, before the party separated to allow its members to inspect the building at their leisure. Sir Marcus approached Lady Rosalyn.

"You look anxious — can I be of assistance?" he asked her.

"I wonder what has become of my nephews — I have not seen them for some time."

"I thought I saw them slip outside a while ago," replied Sir Marcus. "Shall we go in search of them?"

Rosalyn allowed him to escort her out of the church, and the sudden brightness made her pause, blinking as she looked around her. Ahead of her, the path led to the main gates, to the right of it the tombstones and monuments stood row by row from the path to the hedge that bounded the church grounds. To the left of the path, the grass lay smooth and unbroken, except for a scattering of young trees.

"I believe the grounds descend to a river on this side. I would guess that is where we should find our quarry," offered Sir Marcus.

He held out his arm for her, and together they strolled along the smaller path which wound down towards a belt of trees at the river-bank.

"I fear John and Charles do not share their mother's interest in Gothic architecture," observed Sir Marcus.

"I do not think it matters, as long as they are enjoying their day."

"And what of you, Lady Rosalyn — are you enjoying your day?"

"Oh, excessively! My spirits are uplifted by the noble edifice man has built in praise of his Creator, and now they are calmed by the delightful tranquillity of this spot!" she replied soulfully.

They turned, following the river's edge, where the trees lined the bank, their branches overhanging and in some places touching the water.

"This reminds me of Helston: the gardens there lead down to a small lake — at least they were used to do so, it may be silted up by now."

"How long since you have seen Helston?"

"Oh, about a year. It needs a fortune to put it to rights — which I do not possess."

He spoke lightly, but Rosalyn was not deceived.

"You are fond of your home, I think."

"Naturally. I was born there, and spent much of my childhood on the estate."

"I should like to see it," Rosalyn said thoughtfully.

They had come to a halt, and she looked up to find Sir Marcus's eyes upon her, a strange glint in them that she could not interpret.

"Perhaps you shall," he murmured.

The sound of boyish laughter recalled them, and Sir Marcus, looking over her head, caught sight of John and Charles engaged in throwing stones into the river.

"There's our quarry, Lady Rosalyn. And if I am not mistaken, that is your dear sister beckoning to them from the rise — it must be time to move on."

Rosalyn called to the boys, and they all set off up the grassy slope to the church gate, where the rest of the party were waiting. Lady Rosalyn encountered a frowning look from Carfax, and she quickly turned to Cynthia to apologise for delaying the party.

"There is plenty of time, Ros. It is not far to the Pelican — we need only to cross the bridge and we are there." Cynthia looked around.

"Now if we are all together, we can go."

"Perhaps, Helston, you would care to escort Miss Penally and her sister," put in Carfax quickly.

Sir Marcus had been about to give his arm to Lady Rosalyn, but at these words he smiled, and turned instead to Miss Penally. "Delighted, sir. Miss Penally, if you would do me the honour — and Miss Diana?"

With a lady on each arm, Sir Marcus led the way out of the church gates. As he passed Lord Carfax he looked up, and as he met that glance Carfax flushed, knowing Helston was aware of his intention to separate him from Lady Rosalyn. After a nudge from his father, Reginald offered his arm to Lady Rosalyn, who accepted this change of escort with complacence, her thoughtful eyes resting for a moment on Mrs. Penally, who was clearly seething with indignation that Carfax should so imperil her daughters' honour. The party made its way at a leisurely pace over the recently widened bridge that spanned the river. This brought them into Milchester's high street, at the far end of which stood the Pelican, where Carfax had arranged for a light repast to be served.

The refreshments were set out in a private parlour, and Damien, having no appetite, took up a position in one corner of the room out of the way of his guests. He was soon joined by Mrs. Penally, whose face wore a disapproving look.

"Well, Carfax, I have no doubt you acted for the best, allowing That Man to escort my girls, but it was effort wasted, I believe." Her eyes travelled to where Lady Rosalyn was pouring coffee, with Sir Marcus standing beside her, smiling at some comment she was making. "I do not doubt the integrity of your sister-in-law," continued Mrs. Penally solemnly, "but I should not wish to see a daughter of mine slipping off alone with a man — but one can only guess what story may have been told to lure that lady away from her party."

"Lady Rosalyn went in search of the children, cousin. I have no reason to doubt her word," replied Carfax shortly.

"I have already given you my opinion," she returned. "I am a little surprised that you have made no effort to remove Sir Marcus from your house — if such a man were to insinuate himself into the favours of my child I would certainly ensure that Mr. Penally made an end to such a liaison as soon as ever possible!"

She said no more, but left Carfax to enjoy his thoughts in solitude.

When his cousin had first raised the matter, Carfax had thought in much the same way as Lady Greenow — that Rosalyn was best left to run her own life (witness the way she had ripped up at him when he had tried to advise her in Town!). But he could not dispel the conviction that she would be making a grave mistake should she ally herself to a penniless rake. During the return journey to Belfort, Damien was unusually silent as he mulled over the problem. In normal circumstances, he would have discussed the matter with Lady Carfax, but circumstances were not normal, and Cynthia gave no indication that she wished to discuss anything with her husband, least of all her sister's actions. In fact she had barely spoken to him all day, and when he had handed her into the carriage she had not even glanced at him, and said her thanks in so stony a voice that there was no mistaking her indifference.

Had he but known it, Lady Carfax was quite as unhappy as her husband; she had noticed his angry looks when he spotted Sir Marcus and Rosalyn in the grounds of the church, and when they had returned to the Pelican she had been most painfully aware of her husband, standing alone and fixedly regarding Lady Rosalyn. Cynthia was much hurt by this behaviour, and for the remainder of the day she was at pains to avoid his company.

Thus Carfax, unwilling to broach the

matter with so distant a wife, spent a restless night deciding whether he should act to prevent what would be, in his opinion, a disastrous alliance between Rosalyn and Sir Marcus. He could not deny that he had been pleasantly surprised in the man — in fact he found that he could not help liking Sir Marcus, but he had led a wild existence, and his reputation for gaming was well known. By morning, Carfax had decided he could be silent no longer, he must at least speak to Sir Marcus. Damien quit his room and went in search of his guest, only to be informed by a servant that Sir Marcus had left the house early with Lord John and Master Charles.

"I believe they were going fishing, my lord," offered the footman. "Mr. Gargeney expects them to return by noon."

"When they come back, inform Sir Marcus that I wish to speak to him," ordered Carfax before shutting himself in his library.

10

THE library at Belfort was an impressive one; the room was large, with every wall holding bookshelves from floor to ceiling, save where the windows broke the lines of leather-bound volumes. Carfax took down a book at random from one of the shelves, hoping to while away the time, but soon he gave up the pretence of reading and threw the book down upon a desk. Damn the fellow, he thought irritably, how could one quarrel with a guest who took such an interest in the boys, much less ask him to leave? Childish laughter in the hallway caught his attention, and he flung open the door of the library, which led directly onto the hall. The two boys stood at the foot of the stairs, with Sir Marcus between them.

"Papa! We have had such good

sport, and we nearly caught *hundreds* of fish!" cried Charles. "Sir Marcus is a prime gun, sir! The best of fishermen — except you, of course, Papa," he added as an afterthought.

"Thank you," said Carfax absently. "Helston, I would like a word with you, if you would spare me but five minutes — "

Sir Marcus followed his host into the library, leaving the children to make their noisy way upstairs.

"You will be relieved to know that we have in no way depleted your stock of fish. Our luck was out, the couple of catches we made were so small that we returned them to the water."

"I am obliged to you."

Carfax stood by his desk, his back to Sir Marcus.

"I wish to talk to you about a very — delicate — matter."

"Indeed?"

"What I have to say concerns Lady Rosalyn."

"I thought that might be the case,"

murmured Sir Marcus, his eyes never leaving Carfax.

Damien turned to face the other man, but after holding his eyes for a few brief seconds, he dropped his gaze to the desk.

"My decision to speak to you upon this matter was not an easy one to make. You must know that I have pondered long on this problem, but I feel that as I am in some way related to the lady I cannot in all conscience remain silent."

"Go on."

"You must know that your attentions to my sister-in-law have not gone unnoticed. I imagine it is unnecessary to tell you that an alliance would be totally unacceptable to her family?"

"Sour grapes, Carfax?" asked Sir Marcus gently. He saw Lord Carfax stiffen and he laughed humourlessly "No, don't call me out, it would cause a most unpleasant scandal."

"She is too far above your touch, Helston. You are not worthy of her."

"I know that." Sir Marcus took out his snuff-box and helped himself to a pinch. "But I do think that the lady is capable of handling her own affairs."

"She is bewitched," Carfax retorted. "Do you realise what her life would be if she married you? Cut off from her family, her friends would pity her; others would laugh up their sleeves to see a Tremayne so debased!"

Sir Marcus did not move. His face was expressionless as Damien's tirade washed over him.

"You paint a very unpleasant picture."

"I have no wish to see Rosalyn ruin herself!"

"Neither have I," replied Sir Marcus in an even tone. "No doubt you think I should remove myself from her vicinity?"

Carfax looked away.

"Yes."

"Very well. I will leave in the morning, with your permission."

Carfax nodded, and Sir Marcus turned to leave the room, closing the door softly behind him. Damien turned to stare out of the window, overlooking the parkland which rolled away to the wood standing out on the horizon. It was a pleasant view, designed to be admired, but today Carfax saw nothing. He was convinced that he had acted for the best, with Rosalyn's interests at heart, and yet he could not still the murmur of doubt which whispered to him that he had been influenced by more than brotherly affection. He shook his head, as though to dispel such thoughts. He had done what he thought right. Helston would be gone by the morrow, and should Rosalyn decide to continue the liaison in Town, that was her own concern, but no-one should say that Carfax had encouraged it.

Later that day Sir Marcus sought out Lady Rosalyn. He found her alone in the morning-room, writing a letter. She looked up and smiled when she saw him.

"I expected you to take to your

bed for the rest of the day, after such an exhausting morning!" Her eyes twinkled with merriment.

"Do you think me such a poor creature?"

"Not at all, but you are unused to children and I find an hour with two such lively ones is sufficient to lay me low! Do you wish to see me? I am writing to Amelia, but I can leave it — "

Sir Marcus sat down, choosing a chair facing the writing-table in order to watch her.

"I am not in a hurry. Pray continue your letter."

"To own the truth, I have told her everything of interest, and shall make you my excuse to cut my letter short. There." She sanded the sheet, and carefully folded it. "Now, what is it you wish to say to me?" she asked, hunting through the drawers of the desk for a seal.

"I have come to tell you that I shall be leaving tomorrow."

Lady Rosalyn paused in the act of sealing her letter.

"This is very sudden," she said, not looking up.

"I am given to impetuous actions, my dear. Charming though your company has been, I have a yearning for the delights of Brighton."

She looked up at him now, hurt and disbelief in her eyes. Sir Marcus averted his gaze.

"Have I — has anyone offended you?" she asked quietly.

"Not at all, but the quiet life is not to my taste."

"I see." Rosalyn finished sealing her letter, her brain in a turmoil. "I shall be — sorry — to see you go."

"That is very flattering, ma'am."

The indifference in his tone made her wince. She rose from her chair, her eyes searching his face, but it was expressionless, his eyes cold and hard.

"Forgive me if I am naïve — perhaps one should expect such behaviour from a rake," she said, a bitter note creeping into her voice.

"You knew my reputation, ma'am."

Lady Rosalyn stared at his stony face and felt her world collapsing around her. She passed a hand across her eyes, saying unsteadily, "Yes, you never lied to me — I suppose I must be thankful for that. When — when do you go?"

"Tomorrow morning. I will inform my host at dinner. I am sure they will be relieved at my departure."

"An understatement, sir. They will be delighted," she retorted, finding strength in anger.

"As you say, madam." Sir Marcus rose and bowed.

He left the room, and Rosalyn sank back on to the chair, trying to collect her scattered wits. There was little resemblance between the laughing carefree companion she had known these past weeks and the cold, indifferent man she had just seen. Something was wrong; at the back of her mind there was an answer, she was sure, but it eluded her.

"Rosalyn, if you have finished your letter, I have asked Damien to frank it — my love, are you ill?" Lady Carfax came sweeping into the room, and she hurried to her sister, placing a tiny hand on Rosalyn's brow. "There is no fever there, I swear, but you are so white."

Rosalyn gazed blankly up at her. "What? Oh — no, Cindy, I am well enough. It is just a headache." She smiled at Cynthia. "You mentioned my letter, I think?"

"Yes, Damien will frank it, when it is ready."

"I have it here."

Rosalyn handed the letter to her sister and hurried out of the room to seek the seclusion of her bedchamber.

Lady Rosalyn was very subdued at dinner, and Cynthia ascribed her manner to the headache, until Sir Marcus announced his intention of leaving. Cynthia's eyes flew to her sister, who kept her own gaze lowered, showing no signs of surprise at this announcement. She suspected a quarrel, until her husband's calm acceptance of the news made her think that he might know something about the matter. She had no opportunity to ask him at dinner, and was obliged to wait until their guests had retired before she could speak to her husband alone.

"Carfax," she said, as he was about to leave the room, "did you know Sir Marcus intended to leave us tomorrow?"

"He mentioned it to me this morning."

"Did you ask him to go?"

"Not directly," Carfax replied. He looked at his wife. "I informed him that the Tremaynes would not look favourably upon his suit. I am right, do you not think?"

Cynthia clasped her hands together, saying anxiously, "Yes, but — do you think it wise to interfere?"

Carfax shrugged. "I considered it necessary." He saw that Cynthia was looking at him strangely, and added roughly, "Would you have your sister married to such a man?"

Cynthia did not reply, and he flung himself out of the room, slamming the door behind him.

"So, Sir Marcus has departed, cousin. I cannot say I am sorry, he is not at all the sort of man I wish my children to know," Mrs. Penally addressed Carfax across the breakfast-table.

He threw his cousin a look of dislike.

"Helston's reputation is grossly exaggerated," he replied shortly.

"Perhaps, but I am happy to think that you took my advice about that man. While he was in this house I could not rest easily in my bed."

"Oh, I am sure *you* had nothing to fear from him," said Rosalyn sweetly, an angry glitter in her eyes.

The sarcasm was lost on Mrs. Penally, who continued, "I own I was surprised to find such a person here, but I have heard it said that such men can insinuate themselves into the most respectable households. At least, cousin, you had the good sense to send him about his business before any harm was done." She rose, saying, "Now, if you will excuse me, cousin Cynthia, I have promised to show your cook how to prepare a leg of mutton. Her way is very well, I am sure, but I use a much better method, with just a hint of rosemary for the flavouring."

There was silence as she left the room. Lady Rosalyn stared across the table at her brother-in-law.

"Is it true?" she said at last. "Did you ask him to leave?"

"Not exactly."

"But you did speak to him — you knew he was going even before he announced his intention at dinner yesterday?"

"Yes."

"Why, Carfax?" Rosalyn sat very still, waiting for the answer.

"I did it for the best." Carfax did

not look up. "You were growing too attached to him."

"So you told him to leave."

"I merely pointed out how disastrous it would be for you to ally yourself to such a one."

Lady Carfax held her breath, looking from her husband to Rosalyn, whose green eyes blazed with anger, and when she spoke, her voice was low and throbbing.

"How *dare* you meddle in my affairs!"

"Believe me, it was for your own good!" he retorted, a dull flush on his cheek.

"For my *good*! What makes you think you know what is best for me?"

"Ros, please." Lady Carfax put her hand on her sister's arm, only to have it shaken off.

"Keep out of this, Cindy!"

"But I am sure Damien acted as he thought right!"

Rosalyn stood up, her angry gaze never leaving Carfax.

"Pray just what did you say to him?" she demanded wrathfully.

"That your family would strongly disapprove the match. As your brother-in-law, I took it upon myself to act for your protection."

"When you married my sister, sir, you gave up all right to protect *me*, and I'll be damned if I let you rule my life!"

"Rosalyn!" shrieked Cynthia, clapping her hands over her ears.

Rosalyn dashed a hand across her eyes, making a visible effort to control her anger.

"Ten years ago I would have given anything for your protection," she said quietly, "but since then I have controlled my own destiny. Put your own house in order before you look to mine, Carfax!" she ended bitterly, and flung herself out of the room.

An hour later Rosalyn was ready to leave. She stood in the hallway, watching the last of her trunks being strapped to her travelling carriage.

"Must you go like this, Ros? Please stay."

Lady Carfax dabbed at her eyes, while Rosalyn watched her compassionately.

"I am sorry, Cindy, truly I am! I cannot remain here."

"But where are you going?"

"To Larchwood, of course. I have been meaning to see it since I first learned it was part of my inheritance."

"But they do not expect you! It could well be derelict."

"Then I shall put up at an inn and think again!" Lady Rosalyn hugged her sister. "Do not worry, my dear, I shall see you again in Town. I promise I shall not let this quarrel part us again for so long."

A liveried servant handed Lady Rosalyn into her coach, the steps were put up and the door firmly shut. Rosalyn smiled down at Cynthia.

"Say goodbye to John and little Charles for me, Cindy. I have grown very fond of them."

"I will. Take care, Rosalyn."

Lady Carrax raised her hand in salute as the carriage pulled away. She watched it disappear from view on the curving tree-lined drive, then turned and walked sadly back into the house.

11

AT the end of summer, Rosalyn returned to Town reluctantly; she had invited Mrs. Windhurst to join her there, and she would not let her down. The improvements at Larchwood were well in hand, and there was little more she could do there until the work was completed. After the fresh green fields of Hertfordshire, she found the Town very drab and depressing, and a prolonged spell of inclement weather did nothing to improve her spirits. Mrs. Windhurst arrived on a typically damp afternoon, and took the earliest opportunity to exclaim at the change in her cousin.

"I left you in high bloom, love, and return to find you looking positively grey!" she stated frankly, as soon as they were alone.

"I am a little tired. There was so

much to be done at Larchwood that it took all my energies. But my industry has been rewarded, I think. My new staff can be relied upon to keep the place in order. I have also purchased a new range for the kitchen, which will please the French cook I have employed."

Amelia smiled. "Goodness, Rosalyn. Such extravagance! Do you mean to make your home there?"

"I shall spend Christmas there, certainly. After that, who knows?"

"I had thought you would spend Christmas with your sister, at Belfort."

There was a pause.

"I think not. The novelty of having my own house has not yet worn off. I am hoping that the major alterations will be completed by then, and I wish to supervise the final decorations myself. But nothing is settled," added the lady, averting her eyes, "I may well go abroad again."

A suspicion that Rosalyn had quarrelled with Lady Carfax entered Amelia's head, but she did not press the matter, preferring to wait and watch.

Once it was known that Lady Rosalyn Tremayne was in Town, the invitations began to flow in. It seemed to Mrs. Windhurst that Rosalyn was determined to accept them all; she threw herself into a round of balls, parties and masquerades with a gaiety Amelia had never known before, and the feverish activity worried Mrs. Windhurst.

It was two weeks before Rosalyn saw Sir Marcus. She was attending a dress-ball with her cousin when she spotted him, his tall figure making him an easy character to recognise. He looked up, as though he had felt her eyes upon him, but apart from a slight bow he made no move to come to her. Rosalyn turned away, refusing to be upset by such a trivial incident. She saw Major Franklyn bearing down upon her, and allowed him to lead her on to the floor for a country dance.

"Lady Rosalyn is in spirits this evening," observed Lady Greenow, sitting beside Mrs. Windhurst at one end of the room.

The widow watched the dancers, a tiny crease between her brows.

"It has been so ever since her return to Town."

"You are concerned about her nevertheless," said Lady Greenow shrewdly.

Mrs. Windhurst nodded. "She is almost too happy — I fear there is some rift between Rosalyn and Carfax."

"You know of course that Helston left Belfort very suddenly?"

"No! I had not heard that." Mrs. Windhurst paused, reflecting, "Well, if they are estranged, I cannot be sorry. One cannot suppose Rosalyn would be happy with such a man."

"Would you prefer to see her wedded to the Major?" inquired Lady Greenow, nodding towards the couple.

"He at least has no need of her fortune! But no," Mrs. Windhurst laughed, "I can think of few more unsuitable partners for my lively cousin!"

Major Franklyn, reviewing the evening

as he was driven home afterwards, was inclined to think that his suit might prove successful. Lady Rosalyn had been more encouraging than ever before. She had stood up with him for two dances, and he had not once had the uncomfortable suspicion that she was laughing at him, as was usually the case. Had anyone told him that my lady was too preoccupied to give more than a mechanical response to his platitudes he would not have believed them. The lively spirit that disturbed him had been lacking that night, and he was convinced Lady Rosalyn would make him a comfortable wife. The thought of a refusal did not enter his mind, and he determined to set out for Worthing on the morrow to discuss the matter with his mama.

For Lady Rosalyn, the round of social activities continued unabated. Mrs. Windhurst watched and wondered as she made her way tirelessly from one party to the next. They met Sir Marcus frequently in company, but apart from a nod of recognition Amelia could detect no sign that either of them wished to resume their former easy friendship. If she had been able to guess the effort it was costing her cousin to keep her eyes from following Sir Marcus when they were together, she would have been seriously worried.

Carfax and his lady had also returned to Town, but it was plain to their friends that all was not well with them. Mr. Stayne appeared to be Cynthia's most frequent escort, and when Rosalyn asked her sister about Damien, she replied airily, "Oh, he prefers to sit at home, like an old man. I have no patience with him and his books — he does nothing but criticise!"

Lady Rosalyn might resent his interference in her own affairs, but she was too fond of Carfax to wish him to lose his wife. She tried to think of some way to bring the couple to their senses, but could hit upon nothing, except a fervent desire to knock their silly heads together!

After a long discussion with Mrs. Franklyn, the Major made up his mind and arrived at Brook Street early one morning to ask for Lady Rosalyn's hand in marriage. Fortune favoured him, for he found the lady at home, and alone, in the morning-room.

"Lady Rosalyn." He bowed low over her hand. "I am fortunate to find you here alone. I wish to speak to you on a most important matter."

Lady Rosalyn motioned him to a seat.

"Shall I ring for refreshment, Major?"

"No, I thank you. You may have been aware that I have been out of Town for the past few days."

Rosalyn had not noticed, but felt it would be impolite to say so.

Not waiting for a reply, he continued, "I have been to see my mother, to discuss the possibility of my taking a wife. The subject was discussed most thoroughly — but I need not go into detail. In short, Lady Rosalyn — " the Major fixed his earnest gaze upon her — "In short, my Mama looks upon you most favourably, and I have come to you today to ask that you make me the happiest of men, and do me the honour of becoming my wife!"

The lady regarded her guest in the liveliest astonishment.

"I am obliged to your Mama for her opinion, but is that the only reason you wish to marry me?"

"You wish me to utter those remarks which are most agreeable to your sex, do you not?" He smiled indulgently. "I have the very highest regard for you, ma'am, as you must know, and it has been in my mind for some time to ask for your hand, but I feared to be precipitate. Mrs. Franklyn, however, feels that marriage would have a steadying effect upon me, and add a sobriety to my advancing years."

Rosalyn's eyes danced, but she replied gravely, "How prudent of your Mama. I am naturally flattered by your offer, Major, but I fear we should not suit."

"You are too modest, ma'am. You will make an admirable wife."

"Perhaps, sir, but I regret that I do not feel for you the warmer emotions that one expects in marriage."

"It may be that I have been too hasty. My proposal has taken you by surprise. A night's reflection will dispel your doubts, I am sure."

"No, Major Franklyn, I do not think so," said Lady Rosalyn gently. She rose from her chair. "I am sorry to disappoint you, sir."

"So too am I, but I will not despair, I have heard that it is often the case that young ladies refuse an offer, only to change their minds at a later date." He smiled at her knowingly. "I shall wait and see," he said comfortably.

The Major took his leave, and as Lady Rosalyn heard the front door close behind him she gave way to her emotions.

"Rosalyn my love, have you seen my — Good heavens, my dear, what is the matter?" Mrs. Windhurst, entering the morning-room, was appalled to find her cousin sitting with her head in her hands.

Lady Rosalyn looked up and began to mop her streaming eyes.

"Major Franklyn has made me an offer!"

"Well, I fail to see why that should send you into hysterics."

"He — he told me that his Mama thought marriage to me would have a — a sobering effect upon him," replied Rosalyn in an unsteady voice.

"Oh! I see." Mrs. Windhurst tried to remain grave, and failed dismally. "Oh, poor man! We should not ridicule him," she said when she could at last command her voice.

"Oh, do not waste your pity on him, Amelia. He is convinced I shall change my mind!"

"I trust you can persuade him that his suit is hopeless."

Lady Rosalyn smiled, saying mischievously, "Perhaps I should commit some indiscretion that will shock Mrs.

Franklyn into reviewing her good opinion of me!"

Despite her levity on this occasion, Mrs. Windhurst found her anxiety for Lady Rosalyn increasing rapidly. She had been shocked when she had first arrived in Brook Street at the end of the summer to see the change in her cousin. There was a brittle quality to her gaiety, and she had lost the fresh bloom that had touched her beauty the previous season. Lady Rosalyn would fall silent for long periods, and when recalled to the present, Mrs. Windhurst thought her chatter just a little too bright.

On fine mornings, Lady Rosalyn would leave the house early to ride in the Park, with Williams, her groom, following behind her in a disapproving silence. He had known Rosalyn since she had been a child; he had seen her angry, and he had known her to be sad, but never before had he known her to be so utterly dejected. If the servants gossip was to be believed (not, of course, that he ever listened to such), my lady was pining for her brother-in-law. Williams was not so sure — he would far rather put his money on the fortune-hunter who had been used to haunt the house at the end of last season. He watched his mistress as she rode before him: it would not last, he told himself grimly. My lady was not one to sit idle in misfortune, but the Lord alone knew what she would do; he could only hope that it would be nothing too outrageous!

It was not long before the strain of her feverish activity began to tell on Rosalyn. She excused herself from a number of parties, preferring to sit at home. There was one event, however, that she would not avoid. Lady Greenow was holding a Dress Ball, and Rosalyn could not disappoint her friend. Mrs. Windhurst urged her to wear her latest gown, but although Rosalyn looked enchanting in the emerald silk, with a lace shawl caught about her shoulders, she lacked the sparkle that had so enhanced her beauty during the spring.

For Lady Greenow, the evening was a great success. The ballroom was overflowing with guests, and they were still arriving! It seemed to Rosalyn that all London was in attendance, certainly everyone she knew. Lord and Lady Carfax arrived together, and Rosalyn thought she had never seen her sister looking lovelier dressed entirely in silver and white. Carfax, too, looked very handsome in his dark blue coat, which seemed moulded to his form, and his necktie creased into intricate folds beneath his chin. She found her gaze wandering to Sir Marcus who, in contrast to her brother-in-law's neat attire, was dressed in his usual careless fashion. No servant was needed to ease him into his coat, and it had been known for arbiters of fashion to shut their eyes at the sight of his carelessly tied cravat.

"Quite a squeeze, eh? My wife is very

satisfied with herself for this crush!" said Sir Ingram, jovially.

Lady Rosalyn smiled. "With good reason, sir. It must rate as one of the best assemblied of the season."

Sir Ingram was well pleased with this tribute, but his gaze was troubled as he looked at his guest.

"Forgive me, ma'am, if I say that you are looking a little pale — I hope you have not been knocking yourself up with all your pleasuring."

"Not at all. I have a headache coming on, I fear."

"I trust it will not be serious, my dear, but if you should wish for a little solitude, my book-room is at your disposal. I always have a fire kindled there for these occasions, so that I can slip away should I wish to do so, but you must feel free to make use of it, Lady Rosalyn."

"Thank you, Sir Ingram," Lady Rosalyn replied gratefully, "I hope it will not be necessary."

Lady Rosalyn's depression did not

lift, and after a couple of hours she felt that she could smile no longer. She slipped out of the ball-room and across the hall. As Sir Ingram had promised, the book-room was empty, with a cheerful fire and the minimum of candles casting a restful glow over the apartment. She closed the door behind her and gave a sigh of relief. She only had time to sit down before the door opened again and Sir Marcus appeared.

"I saw you leave the ball-room."

She smiled a little.

"I need relief from the noise and heat. Lady Greenow has excelled herself tonight."

He picked up a lighted candelabra from the side table, crossed the room, and stood looking down at her, frowning.

"You are not well," he said bluntly. "Do you wish me to call your cousin?"

"No. Stay and talk to me." She saw him hesitate, and put up her hand to touch his sleeve. "Please."

He set down the candles.

"As you wish, ma'am."

"I thought I saw Boston riding that showy chestnut of yours yesterday."

"It is most likely that you did." Sir Marcus studied his reflection in the large mirror above the fireplace. He put up a hand to adjust a fold in his neckcloth.

"I sold her to pay off some of my creditors." He spoke lightly.

"Are things that bad, then?"

"A slight reverse, merely. I shall come about again."

Lady Rosalyn drew a breath.

"There is one way out of your difficulties — a more permanent way."

"Marriage? Perhaps, as a last resort. I am not ready for that yet."

She rose and stood behind him. In the mirror their eyes met, and she said steadily,

"My fortune is large enough for us both, Marcus."

"No!" He swung round, his hands catching her shoulders roughly. "Lady

256

Rosalyn Tremayne, from one of the oldest and most respected families in the country, to ally herself to a penniless gambler? Good God, do you know what people would say?"

She met his gaze squarely.

"I care not what they say." A smile touched her lips. "You must not forget your aunt's fortune."

"Would that make my conduct any less despicable? To marry you in order to gain her favour?"

"But she approves of me," replied Rosalyn with a touch of humour. She kept her eyes on his face. "You would have married me, once."

"That was before I knew you."

"And now?"

He turned away from her. When he spoke his voice was harsh.

"Now my regard for you is such that I could never marry you — you are too far above me."

"Did Damien tell you that?"

"He did not need to — I have known it for some time."

She moved closer to him. He stood with his back to her, and she put her hand gently upon his arm.

"You know how I feel, Marcus. I am ready to put my happiness in your hands — God knows I can find none without you."

"You will recover," he replied shortly.

She withdrew her hand as though she had been stung.

"Another ten years of loneliness!" she cried savagely. "Is that how you would have me live?"

Helston turned suddenly, and pulled her roughly into his arms.

"Ah don't — love! How can I bear to see you cry?" he murmured huskily, burying his face in her hair. She clung to him, her own face turned in to his shoulder.

His hold slackened, and she looked up into his face, tears sparkling on her lashes.

"Marcus, all I have is yours — it means nothing to me without you." She gave a shaky laugh. "I sound like the heroine of some dreadful melodrama, do I not?"

He did not smile, but stared down at her for a long moment. Lady Rosalyn saw his mouth set in a determined line and he put her away from him.

"No," he said quietly. "You say that now, Rosalyn, but you will thank me one day for not marrying you, believe me."

She gazed up at him, her eyes searching his face. After a moment, she sighed and shook her head.

"You are resolved."

"Yes."

"Even though you love me?"

"Even though — I love you."

She smiled sadly.

"What can I say? You are so sure you know what is best for me — I wonder if there is anyone who believes that I know my own mind best?"

He remained silent. With a slight shrug of her white shoulders Rosalyn put out her hand.

"I shall go home now, I think. May

I still call you friend, Sir Marcus?"

He raised her hand to his lips, his eyes fixed on her face.

"Indeed you may, my lady."

"Then goodnight, my friend." She smiled up at him briefly, then turned and left the room.

12

EVERYONE was agreed that lady Greenow's Dress Ball had been a great success, and Mrs. Windhurst, taking a dish of tea with her friend a week later, was able to report that she had heard nothing but praise for the occasion from all she met.

"What a pity Rosalyn had to leave so early. I do hope her malaise has not developed into anything more serious than the headache?"

"No. She was quite well by the morning. It is most strange, but for the past week my cousin has seemed far more — content, if that is the correct word. She is certainly thoughtful, but I have the oddest feeling that she is a great deal happier."

"I am glad of it. It is to be hoped, then, that she had suffered no lasting injury from her encounter with Sir

Marcus Helston?"

Mrs. Windhurst nodded.

"I thought for a time they would make a match of it, but I cannot be sorry that it has come to nothing. I can now be more comfortable again."

It was as well that Mrs. Windhurst was unable to read her cousin's thoughts, for she would then have been far from comfortable. Lady Rosalyn considered the reasons Sir Marcus had given for not marrying her were quite trivial, but she could appreciate his concern; now that she was sure he returned her affection, she was determined to hit upon a way to bring him round to her way of thinking.

She was with Mrs. Windhurst when the idea first occurred to her. They were enjoying a peaceful evening at home, and Amelia was engaged in knotting a fringe. That lady was suddenly startled to hear her cousin laugh.

"Is anything the matter, love?" she asked anxiously.

"No, Amelia, I was merely remembering an old joke."

Mrs. Windhurst looked at her enquiringly, but Rosalyn shook her head.

"No, I shall not tell you, Amelia," she said, her eyes twinkling, "I doubt it would amuse you."

Amelia did not press the matter, but it was clear to Lady Rosalyn that her cousin was intrigued.

"Did you not meet my sister today, Amelia? I recollect you were engaged to have tea with her," said Rosalyn, changing the subject.

"Yes, I saw her. I fear she is not happy, Rosalyn. That man Mr. Stayne called as I was leaving."

"You do not like him, Amelia?"

"He is very personable, but there is a cold, calculating look in his eyes that gives one pause. I own I *cannot* like him, but I may be wrong — I know very little of the man, after all."

"I, too, mistrust him, cousin. I would that my sister dropped that connection."

"From something Cynthia said to me it would appear that Carfax is beginning to show his disapproval."

"Does it? Well, I hope Damien will send him about his business, for I fear that man will make mischief if he can. Oh, by the by, I shall not be able to accompany you tomorrow, I have remembered I have some business to attend to that will not wait."

"How tiresome for you, love. Is there anything I can do to help?"

"Thank you, no, Amelia. I shall be engaged most of the day."

The following morning, as soon as Mrs. Windhurst had left the house on a shopping expedition, Rosalyn summoned her groom. When he arrived he found his mistress busily writing a letter.

"Ah, Williams. Have you a reliable lad you can send out of Town today?"

"Aye, my lady, young Thomas can go."

"Good. I want him to take this letter — tell him to wait for a reply. If it is favourable I shall need my curricle here by ten tomorrow morning, is that understood?"

He took the letter.

"Yes, my lady."

"Oh, and Williams."

"Yes, ma'am?"

"I believe you have a brother in Town?"

"That is correct, my lady. He runs a tavern in Holborn."

"Do you think he could find me two men? Strong fellows, Williams, who could be trusted?"

The groom looked surprised.

"If the price is right, Lady Rosalyn. May I ask what you would be wanting with two such men?"

"You may, but I will not tell you!" Her eyes twinkled. "Suffice to say that my purpose is within the law. Well, almost," she added truthfully.

"If it's havey-cavey business you are about, my lady, then I won't help you do it!" declared the groom sternly.

"Of course you will! You always do

265

what I want," she replied confidently.

She saw the stubborn set of his chin and said coaxingly, "I promise you it is quite a small task I have for them; merely to protect me from a certain gentleman, should the need arise."

"May I suggest that you use two of your own footmen, ma'am? I feel sure they will prove adequate."

"No doubt, but my mind is made up. I require two men — two burly individuals. If you will not oblige me, Williams, then I shall have to hire them myself — I am sure I could find many such types willing to aid me at the nearest tavern."

The groom blanched at the idea of Lady Rosalyn entering a rowdy gin house, and he capitulated. He was rewarded with a blinding smile.

"I knew you would not fail me! Now, have Thomas deliver that letter and return an answer to me with all speed."

Having received the answer she expected, Lady Rosalyn set out from

Brook Street promptly at ten o'clock the next morning. As she turned into New Bond Street, she saw her brother-in-law walking a short distance ahead. Rosalyn pulled her team to a halt beside the flagway.

"Good morning, Carfax. Are you going far? Can I take you up?"

Lord Carfax was surprised by the unusually friendly greeting, and he hesitated.

"I have an appointment in the City — Cheapside."

"Then it is no problem — I can go that way."

Carfax climbed up beside her, and they moved off, neither of them aware that a gentleman on the far side of the road was watching them intently.

"You are about early today," observed Carfax.

"I am visiting a friend who lives near Brasted — on the Tonbridge Road."

"A long way — do you intend to stay overnight?"

"No. I do not mean to press my

horses, but we shall be back in time for dinner."

There was silence as Lady Rosalyn gave her attention to the team, who showed a tendency to shy at the sight of an approaching wagon. When they were safely passed, Carfax spoke.

"Ros, I wish to apologise — "

"There is no need."

"I had no right to interfere with your happiness."

"Thank you. It is done, however, and no good can come of reviving the subject. Tell me instead how my sister does."

He laughed bitterly.

"I hardly see her."

"If I may offer you a word of advice, Carfax. Keep her away from Richard Stayne."

"I have asked her to see less of him. What more can I do? I fear that if I should forbid her to see him at all, she will defy me."

They were passing St. Paul's by this time, and Lady Rosalyn was unable to say anything more to Carfax before she set him down. She then drove on, crossed the river and soon left the City behind her.

When Lady Rosalyn arrived at Duffley, the Dowager Duchess of Kendle was alone, awaiting her arrival in her small sitting-room.

"I was surprised to get your letter," said the Dowager bluntly, not allowing her guest time to speak.

"I should not have troubled you, had the case not been so desperate."

Lady Rosalyn was motioned towards a chair, and she sat down before continuing, "It concerns your nephew and godson, ma'am — he has told me that you wish him to marry."

"I do, and should he marry to please me I shall leave him my fortune, which will be no inconsiderable sum."

Lady Rosalyn flushed slightly, but fixed her frank gaze upon her hostess.

"Would you object if he married me?"

"You?" The Dowager was startled.

"I should of course consider it a most suitable match, from Helston's point of view."

"You see, ma'am, I am in love with Sir Marcus, and he returns my regard, but he has made up his mind that he is not good enough for me, that it would ruin me to marry him."

"That sounds unusually noble of Marcus, Lady Rosalyn."

"I know, but it is true. I cannot convince him that I do, truly, wish to marry him."

"If he has no wish to wed you, my dear, then I should forget him. You cannot force him into wedlock."

"In any other case I would agree with you, but he has taken to gambling very heavily, and I fear that if something is not done, and quickly, he will have to fly the country to avoid his creditors."

"My dear girl! You must be mad!" declared the Dowager.

Lady Rosalyn smiled.

"No, your Grace, I am not mad, but I am willing to risk all to prove that Sir

Marcus and I can be happy."

The old lady stared at her guest, as though trying to read her mind. At last she said abruptly,

"Very well. What is it you wish of me?"

Lady Rosalyn drove back to Town very well satisfied with the result of her visit. The Dowager had insisted that she modify her plan somewhat, but she had expected that. In fact, she had been more than a little afraid that when she outlined her intentions the old lady might order her from her the house, instead of which the Dowager had found the whole thing highly amusing! It was decided that the plan should be put into action in two days' time. It would mean Rosalyn would have to cry off from Lady Beezley's party, but that would not be difficult. She determined to finalise her arrangements very carefully; she was gambling with her happiness, and wanted no mistakes.

Lady Carfax, reclining on an elegant

sofa in the Blue Salon, closed her book with something like a snap, and put it on the table at her elbow. A silly novel, it was giving her the headache. She closed her eyes for a moment, trying to shut out the sound of a bell pealing somewhere in the house. A moment later, the door opened. Lady Carfax, opening one eye, sat up with a small shriek.

"Richard! You should not be here! You know Carfax does not like you to visit me at home!"

"I saw him leave, dearest, and took the opportunity of seeing you."

He knelt before her, smiling. Lady Carfax gave a faint, trembling smile in return before looking away.

"Oh, Richard, I am so unhappy!" She pulled at her small, lacy handkerchief with unsteady fingers. "We had words this morning, and Carfax has told me I must not see you again, or he will send me back to Belfort!"

"How could he! No-one who really cared for you would wish to see you incarcerated in such a way!"

He took her hand and pressed it.

"It must not be, Cynthia!"

She jumped up and took a hasty turn about the room.

"I could not bear to live there permanently! How could Damien be so cruel?"

"It would free him to enjoy Lady Rosalyn's company, would it not?"

She stopped her perambulations, and shook her head at him.

"That is over. Rosalyn has assured me there is nothing between them."

"Did you not know your husband was meeting her yesterday?"

"No. He was on business in the City. You must be mistaken."

Mr. Stayne shook his head, saying gently, "I saw them myself, madam. Driving through New Bond Street."

"I cannot believe it!" cried Cynthia in amazement. "There must be an explanation!"

"I wish there were, ma'am, but if you had seen them — " He stopped, watching the effect of his words upon her.

She returned to the sofa and sank down, her face pale. He knelt before her.

"You must not let him send you away, my love!"

"But what can I do?"

"Let me take you away with me. If Carfax wants you out of the way, at least we shall be together. I love you, Cynthia, and I will cherish you as you deserve!"

"But — but what of my children? They are at Belfort. I would never be allowed to see them again."

"Then we will take them with us. I have always wanted a family."

"You have?" She looked at him wonderingly.

"But of course," Mr. Stayne lied easily. He put his arms around her. "How soon can you be ready? I cannot bear to leave you another hour in this house!"

"Not yet!" Cynthia pulled herself

away, shaken by his impetuosity.

"We must lose no time, my darling! Carfax may carry out his threat at any moment!"

"I am not sure — oh, it cannot be tonight! We are holding a card-party, and I could not leave Damien to face that — only think of the scandal!"

Mr. Stayne curbed his exasperation.

"Then it must be tomorrow."

"Oh, — "

He put a finger to her lips. "No, give me no more excuses, ma'am. If you don't wish to come with me, tell me so now, and I will not trouble you again."

Cynthia drew out her lace-edged handkerchief and wiped her eyes.

"How can you say that? It is just — "

"Then you must be ready to fly with me tomorrow night. My coach will be waiting close by at eleven-thirty — can you steal away unnoticed?"

Cynthia nodded dejectedly.

He ignored her palpable lack of enthusiasm, and took her in his arms, murmuring his plans for the future into her ear.

"We can go abroad, my love. I will show you Venice, take you to Florence and Rome — we may even buy a house there! Say you will come, Cindy!"

"Yes, I will come," she whispered miserably.

Her response was not as enthusiastic as he had hoped, but he was satisfied.

"Until tomorrow, then," he said, kissing her hand.

Lady Rosalyn rose early on Thursday morning, aware of a mounting excitement within her. She was surprised and not a little alarmed when her groom arrived at the house, requesting to see her.

"Well, Williams, what is it?" she began, as he was shown in. "Has something gone wrong with our plans?"

The groom tugged at his forelock respectfully.

"No, m'lady, in fact, you may not think it concerns you at all."

"Get on with it, man! I have a great deal to do this morning."

Williams looked uncomfortable.

"Well, ma'am, it's like this. You remember you told me to hire for you two — er — servants? My brother brought two likely ones to me, and last night I went to the Merry Dog to blow a cloud, and to give these two coves their orders for tonight. Well, ma'am, there was a noisy crowd in the corner, coachmen in the main, with one or two others. They was all well-oiled, and one of 'em starts telling his cronies not to look for 'im for a while, since 'is master is leaving Town tonight with a lady — a married lady, ma'am."

Rosalyn grew pale as a suspicion grew in her mind.

"Go on.?"

The man looked down at the carpet.

"The coachman is Mr. Stayne's man, my lady."

"Merciful Heavens! Let us be blunt, Williams. You think this involves my sister?"

"There have been rumours, ma'am, yes."

Rosalyn sank down on to a chair, one hand pressed to her temple.

"Oh, dear God, why tonight of all nights?" she whispered. She thought quickly, then crossed to a writing-desk and drew out a sheet of paper. "You must take this note to Carfax immediately," she ordered, her pen flying across the paper. "Take it yourself, and make sure you give it directly to Lord Carfax, and none other."

Twenty minutes later he was back, with the information that Lord and Lady Carfax were not at home, and were not expected until late.

"Then perhaps you have it wrong, mayhap it is not my sister who is involved," mused Rosalyn, not unhopefully. She saw his sceptical expression and threw out her hands. "What am I to do?" she cried. "What if I am wrong — can you imagine the harm I could do by telling Carfax of my suspicions?" She took a turn about the room, her brain racing. "They are engaged to Lady Beezley tonight, I know. Well, there is no help for it, I must go there, and if my sister is not present — well, we shall see what can be done."

"Does that mean you are cancelling your other plans for this night, my lady?" enquired Williams, hopefully.

"Not at all. A slight alteration is all that is needed, I trust."

She saw his face drop, and could not suppress a smile.

"Don't look so disapproving, Williams. If we are successful I shall soon be a respectable married lady."

"Aye, and if not we shall all end in Newgate," he returned gloomily.

13

LORD and Lady Beezley's town house was ablaze with light. The road leading past the entrance was choked with carriages, each one in turn depositing its gorgeously gowned occupants at the foot of the shallow steps that led to the open doorway, before driving off to make way for the next. Rosalyn was in glowing looks, and several friends complimented her upon her appearance. She had dressed with unusual care, choosing a gown of her favourite green, décolleté and trimmed with snow-white lace. Matching gloves and slippers completed the picture, and Mrs. Windhurst, fondly observing her cousin, thought she had never looked lovelier.

Major Franklyn, coming up to Rosalyn early in the evening, said very much the same thing, adding, with an almost ardent glow in his serious eyes, "I have not given up hope that I shall eventually be successful in my suit, dear Lady Rosalyn, and seeing your radiant beauty tonight only strengthens my resolve to persevere."

"I wish you would not, Major," she replied earnestly. "It can only bring you disappointment, and there are ladies far worthier to be your wife."

The Major smiled complacently.

"Nothing you can say or do will convince me of that, ma'am. You stand too high in my esteem!"

Lady Rosalyn smiled.

"We shall see!" she murmured almost to herself.

"By the by," Major Franklyn lowered his voice a little, "I am so glad to see that that fellow Helston is no longer hanging around you. I hear at the clubs that he is quite done up, you know. Not at all the sort of person for your ladyship to be seen with."

Rosalyn's smile grew wider.

"Indeed? It is strange, but despite his

impecunious state, Sir Marcus is one of the most interesting gentlemen of my acquaintance!" she said sweetly, and walked off leaving the Major wondering if he had in some way offended her.

Rosalyn soon spotted Carfax, and her heart sank when she realised her sister was not one of his party. As soon as she could she approached him and drew him aside.

"Damien, where is Cindy?"

"She was not feeling well, and has gone home."

"But you have seen her today?"

He looked surprised.

"Of course. We spent the day with the Cairns, but after dinner Cynthia went on home — she looked so poorly I wanted to go with her, but she insisted I remain with Lord Cairn's party. What is the matter? Why do you look at me in that way?" asked Carfax, suddenly alarmed.

Rosalyn clasped his arm.

"You must go home at once, Carfax. Cindy — I have reason to believe that

Cynthia is planning to run off, with Richard Stayne."

He froze, the colour draining from his face. When at last he spoke, his voice was indifferent, controlled.

"It has come, then."

Rosalyn shook his arm impatiently.

"Don't be absurd, Damien! You must put a stop to it!"

"What would be the point? If she prefers him to me — "

"Fiddle! Cynthia may think he loves her more than you do, and I have no doubt at all that you have thrown her at him, with your cold looks — I would wager that instead of playing the ardent lover you have taken the rôle of autocratic husband!" She saw from his expression that her conjecture was correct, and pressed home her point. "For God's sake, Damien," she said urgently, "if you have any feeling at all for my sister you will go to her immediately: you cannot let her make such a disastrous mistake!"

He stared at her earnest countenance

for a long moment, then without another word he turned and strode off.

Sitting alone in her room, Cynthia stared dejectedly into her mirror. She could not recall having spent a more miserable day; she had tried to store every moment of it in her memory, since it was the last time she would ever see Damien. The thought was so lowering that she had very little appetite for her dinner, and was so obviously out of spirits that it took very little effort to convince everyone that she should not go to Lady Beezley's party. The worst of it had been Damien's concern, which had brought her close to tears, but she begged him to go on without her, to give her excuses to Lady Beezley. This will not do, she scolded herself. It must be close on eleven, and she had not even put on her dress; if she continued to dwell on Damien's kindness she would never go. Better to remember that he did not love her, that he wanted Ros; yes, that was much more to the point, for it made her wish she was dead!

She heard the door open and turned, expecting to see her abigail.

"Oh!" she gasped, startled. "Carfax! I — you are home early. I did not expect to see you for hours yet."

She cast an anxious look towards the bed, where her gown and travelling-cloak were laid out, but Carfax did not appear to notice.

"Did you not?" asked Carfax, seating himself upon the wooden chest in one corner of the room. "I was concerned for you, and came home early to see you."

"How — how kind of you to say so. I was about to go to bed."

He ignored the hint, and continued to sit on the chest, watching her.

"Perhaps a change of air would do you good. Would you like me to take you to Bath for a few weeks? Do you remember how much we enjoyed ourselves when we went there soon after our wedding? How we laughed at the people in the Pump Room, screwing up their faces as they took the waters?"

Cynthia blinked rapidly. How cruel of him to remind her of such happy days when she knew they were gone for ever.

"We — we will talk of it in the morning, if you please," she said, "I am very tired."

Carfax did not appear to hear her, and continued to reminisce. The clock in the hall struck the hour, but Cynthia did not hear it. She sat very still, staring into space. Watching her carefully, Carfax allowed his words to tail away; her eyes filled with tears, and as they spilled over onto her pale cheeks he said quietly,

"Don't go, Cindy."

Her eyes flew to his face, then she hid her face in her hands. In a moment he was beside her, cradling her in his arms as she cried.

"I did not want to go," she sobbed,

clinging to him. "I thought — I thought you — "

"I know, dearest," he murmured, kissing her hair. "It was my fault for not telling you how desperately I love you."

With a little cry of happiness she threw her arms around his neck, and they clung together. At last she pushed him away a little.

"But what shall I do — he will be waiting."

"I shall take care of that for you, my dear."

She saw his grim look and exclaimed, "You must not call him out, Carfax, you might be hurt!"

He kissed her.

"I won't do that, but we shall let him kick his heels until morning — he can wait all night, for all I care — and then he will receive a note which will make it sufficiently clear that it would be wise for him to remove from Town for a while."

Cynthia gave a shuddering sigh and

laid her head on his shoulder.

"I have been so foolish."

"We both have, love."

He kissed her again, and swore in exasperation when a servant scratched upon the door and timidly announced that Mrs. Windhurst was below and very desirous to see my lord.

"Very well," said my lord, "you had best send her up."

Mrs. Windhurst came in and stopped abruptly in the doorway.

"You may feel free to speak, cousin," said Carfax, with a smile at his wife. "There are no secrets between us."

"I am very glad to hear it," declared the widow. She handed a letter to him. "I thought perhaps you could throw a little light on this."

"What is it, Damien?" asked Cynthia, peeping over his shoulder.

"It's from Rosalyn," explained Carfax, quickly scanning the sheet. "She says she will be staying with friends for a while, and not to worry about her."

"But people do not decide to leave a

party at eleven o'clock at night and visit friends," objected Mrs. Windhurst.

"It is unlikely, but not inconceivable," returned Carfax with a shrug.

Mrs. Windhurst wrung her hands.

"I know something dreadful has happened!" she cried. "She has been so unhappy recently. What if she has decided to end it all?"

"Not Rosalyn," stated Carfax firmly, a ghost of a smile on his lips. "It's not only her green eyes that remind one of a cat — she will always land on her feet, whichever way she goes. Go home and do as she says, Amelia. Rosalyn knows what she is about."

If Lady Rosalyn could have heard his words she would have been considerably heartened. Sitting in her travelling carriage outside a certain club in St. James's Street, she felt a shiver of apprehension run through her as her note was handed to the porter. Perhaps Sir Marcus had already left the club, or would not answer her urgent summons. No, if he was there, she did not doubt he would come if he thought her in trouble. Her heart beat fast as she saw his familiar figure silhouetted against the lighted doorway. He stepped briskly towards the coach and jumped in without a moment's pause. The coach was already moving before he realised he was not alone. He peered across the darkened carriage.

"Lady Rosalyn! What mad start is this?" His tone was amused. "Your note said you were in urgent need of my help."

"I hoped that might persuade you to come with me."

"And how may I help you, ma'am?"

His voice was cool, but her next words shook him out of his unusually polite manner.

"I wish you to marry me."

There was a pause. When Sir Marcus spoke, his voice was harsh.

"I thought we had already discussed that matter."

"We have, sir, and I do not intend to

renew my arguments. I have kidnapped you instead."

"You have what?" He burst out laughing. "Rosalyn, you wretch! You cannot be serious!"

"Never more so. You see, Marcus, everyone has persuaded you that you are totally unsuitable for me, and you have been so distant — what else could one do to persuade you that I really do wish to marry you?"

"You are wrong, my girl!" he retorted bitterly. "I know very well you want to marry me, but it would be wrong of me to take advantage of you in such a way."

"You talk as though I were a child fresh from the schoolroom."

"In this case you are just that! Do you wish the whole town to say I married you for your fortune? It would be the truth, my dear," he added brutally, "the only reason for my attentions was your wealth."

"At the start, perhaps, Marcus. But if that were still so, you would not cry off so readily now. That is why I have abducted you," she ended sunnily.

"Either you call a halt to this silly business or I shall do so! I will not let you ruin yourself like this!"

He put his head out of the carriage and called to the coachman to pull up; the pace did not slacken.

"Do not waste your energies, sir. I am paying these men highly for their — ah — 'specialised' services, and with your own fortune so depleted I doubt if you could bribe them."

"Witch," he flung at her, as he settled himself into one corner. "Where are you taking me?" he enquired conversationally, some time later.

"That I shall not tell you, except that since we have crossed the Thames you will know it will not be Gretna! It is an isolated spot, and I shall keep you there until you agree to marry me, which I trust will not be long, for if you resist I must set it about that *you* ran off with *me*, and have compromised me in the most shocking way — I am sure no-one will doubt my word," she told him in a comfortable tone.

He laughed, genuinely amused.

"Oh, Ros, my beautiful idiot! What would you do if I take it into my head to jump out of this carriage? We are not too far from London — I could make it there by morning. Or perhaps I should just use force to make you order this coach to turn about?" he suggested cordially.

"I think I should warn you, my love, that my men were not hired solely for their ability to handle horses, and they have already been instructed what to do in such an event," came the calm reply.

The gentleman gave an exasperated sigh.

"You cannot be serious about continuing this charade, your reputation will be ruined."

"If you love me as much as you profess, then you will promise to marry me, and save me from myself," she pointed out.

She found herself suddenly seized by the shoulders as Sir Marcus moved across the coach to sit beside her.

"Do you not realise that it is *because* I love you that I cannot marry you?"

"I understand you are afraid you will make me unhappy, that you are not the right man for me. Well, I believe you are the only husband for me, but I do *not* intend to remain single for the next twenty years to prove it!"

He gave a shaky laugh.

"My darling, how can I convince you that you would be better off without me?"

"You will never do that! I have heard all the arguments against you, and to me they appear quite nonsensical. You see, your past life does not worry me, and as for the future — well," she tried for a lighter note, "my fortune need not pass entirely out of my hands upon marriage — I shall ensure I have enough to set up an establishment of my own should I want to do so."

They were driving through open

country now, and the moonlight was bright enough for her to see his face; it seemed to Rosalyn that her love was about to capitulate. She held her breath, but Sir Marcus threw himself back into the corner. With a tiny sigh she settled back, hoping that a little more reflection might make him realise she was in earnest.

The coach rattled on, it's occupants wrapped in their own thoughts.

After a while Sir Marcus asked in his usual calm voice, "What do you intend to do when we arrive at our destination?"

"I have no idea," she replied candidly. "I have never abducted anyone before, but I am sure you will know how to go on," she added comfortably.

"Thank you." His tone was dry, accepting her assumption of his depravity without flinching.

"In any event," she continued, "it does not really matter. After we have spent one night together in the same house, the honourable course for you to take will be to marry me."

"You have forgotten one thing, madam," he retorted. "My reputation is such that it could be almost expected that I would *not* wed you! It has not been my habit to tamper with innocents, but that is about the only sin I have *not* committed!"

Rosalyn felt a cold chill inside her, but she refused to be discouraged. She pretended to consider the point.

"Then I shall retire to some country fastness and live in seclusion. With my fortune I need not marry, but I have no doubt that after such a scandal my family would prefer me to live out of the way — I would be a continual embarrassment in Town, would I not?" She paused before going on slowly, "You see, Marcus, you may be prepared to give up your happiness to protect mine, but I have no intention of letting you ruin my life without at least *attempting* to make you see reason."

"Oh, my God." He reached out

and took her hands. In the gloom his voice sounded strained. "Do you not see what it would mean? My life has been far from perfect: my estates are mortgaged to the hilt — we would provide the Ton with a surfeit of gossip!"

"Fustian!" she replied in a bracing tone. "Many men marry a fortune — worse still most have very little regard for their partners. A protracted stay in the country should prove an ideal honeymoon and I have no doubt that when we return to London some other scandal will have pushed our minor affairs into the shade." She pressed his hands, her eyes straining to see his face. "As to mortgages, my man of business will deal with them, although you will of course have the expectancy of your Godmother's fortune, and if you wish it the main part of my own inheritance can be settled on our children."

She heard him draw a long breath.

"You are a shameless, unscrupulous

hussy, and totally devoid of all morals!" he told her severely.

"Then we shall make a good team, shall we not?"

Sir Marcus dragged her to him and kissed her roughly.

"And if I agree to your preposterous scheme, you will turn this carriage around?" he demanded, still holding her closely.

"First you must promise to wed me, sir."

He held her away from him, trying to read her face.

"Very well," he said at last, "I promise."

Rosalyn gave a sigh of relief and laid her head upon his shoulder.

"Oh, thank Heaven for that!"

"Now will you have this damn — dashed vehicle turn about?"

"Oh, it is much too late to go back to Town tonight. We must be very nearly at Duffley by now."

"Duffley!" Sir Marcus sat up. "Do you mean to tell me that my aunt was a party to your madcap schemes?"

"But of course! Since you have such an aversion to my fortune, I felt the least I could do was to secure hers for you."

"You are too kind," he mocked, adding, "But tell me, whose idea was this 'abduction'?"

"Oh, that was mine, only the Dowager insisted that I bring you to her. She said that if I could not persuade you to wed me by the time we reached Duffley she would see to it that my reputation was protected. She did not think it wise for me to ruin myself totally in the eyes of the world."

"Very good of her."

"You are angry. Do you wish to withdraw from the marriage, Marcus?" she asked him in a small voice.

"No. I was merely considering how lightly I have come off — according to rumour, my aunt married her husband whilst holding a pistol to his head."

Rosalyn gave a gurgle of laughter.

"Really? What an admirable idea! Why did I not think of that?"

"Don't think, madam," he declared awfully, "that now I have agreed to marry you I shall stand for any more of your hoydenish tricks! *I* shall decide when the ceremony will take place, and it will be shrouded in a positive *cloud* of respectability!"

"Of course, Marcus," she replied meekly.

Through the gloom she could see his eyes glinting down at her.

"I was greatly misled by those who said you were far too good for me. I have since discovered that you are an unprincipled baggage, utterly lacking in modesty. You are also headstrong, wilful and thoroughly shameless!"

Unaccountably pleased with this style of address, Rosalyn allowed him to pull her into his arms once more, even going so far as to return his embrace, just to substantiate his opinion.

Other titles in the
Linford Romance Library:

A YOUNG MAN'S FANCY
Nancy Bell

Six people get together for reasons of their own, and the result is one of misunderstanding, suspicion and mounting tension.

THE WISDOM OF LOVE
Janey Blair

Barbie meets Louis and receives flattering proposals, but her reawakened affection for Jonah develops into an overwhelming passion.

MIRAGE IN THE MOONLIGHT
Mandy Brown

En route to an island to be secretary to a multi-millionaire, Heather's stubborn loyalty to her former flatmate plunges her into a grim hazard.

WITH SOMEBODY ELSE
Theresa Charles

Rosamond sets off for Cornwall with Hugo to meet his family, blissfully unaware of the shocks in store for her.

A SUMMER FOR STRANGERS
Claire Hamilton

Because she had lost her job, her flat and she had no money, Tabitha agreed to pose as Adam's future wife although she believed the scheme to be deceitful and cruel.

VILLA OF SINGING WATER
Angela Petron

The disquieting incidents that occurred at the Vatican and the Colosseum did not trouble Jan at first, but then they became increasingly unpleasant and alarming.

DOCTOR NAPIER'S NURSE
Pauline Ash

When cousins Midge and Derry are entered as probationer nurses on the same day but at different hospitals they agree to exchange identities.

A GIRL LIKE JULIE
Louise Ellis

Caroline absolutely adored Hugh Barrington, but then Julie Crane came into their lives. Julie was the kind of girl who attracts men without even trying.

COUNTRY DOCTOR
Paula Lindsay

When Evan Richmond bought a practice in a remote country village he did not realise that a casual encounter would lead to the loss of his heart.

ENCORE
Helga Moray

Craig and Janet realise that their true happiness lies with each other, but it is only under traumatic circumstances that they can be reunited.

NICOLETTE
Ivy Preston

When Grant Alston came back into her life, Nicolette was faced with a dilemma. Should she follow the path of duty or the path of love?

THE GOLDEN PUMA
Margaret Way

Catherine's time was spent looking after her father's Queensland farm. But what life was there without David, who wasn't interested in her?

HOSPITAL BY THE LAKE
Anne Durham

Nurse Marguerite Ingleby was always ready to become personally involved with her patients, to the despair of Brian Field, the Senior Surgical Registrar, who loved her.

VALLEY OF CONFLICT
David Farrell

Isolated in a hostel in the French Alps, Ann Russell sees her fiancé being seduced by a young girl. Then comes the avalanche that imperils their lives.

NURSE'S CHOICE
Peggy Gaddis

A proposal of marriage from the incredibly handsome and wealthy Reagan was enough to upset any girl — and Brooke Martin was no exception.

A DANGEROUS MAN
Anne Goring

Photographer Polly Burton was on safari in Mombasa when she met enigmatic Leon Hammond. But unpredictability was the name of the game where Leon was concerned.

PRECIOUS INHERITANCE
Joan Moules

Karen's new life working for an authoress took her from Sussex to a foreign airstrip and a kidnapping; to a real life adventure as gripping as any in the books she typed.

VISION OF LOVE
Grace Richmond

When Kathy takes over the rundown country kennels she finds Alec Stinton, a local vet, very helpful. But their friendship arouses bitter jealousy and a tragedy seems inevitable.

CRUSADING NURSE
Jane Converse

It was handsome Dr. Corbett who opened Nurse Susan Leighton's eyes and who set her off on a lonely crusade against some powerful enemies and a shattering struggle against the man she loved.

WILD ENCHANTMENT
Christina Green

Rowan's agreeable new boss had a dream of creating a famous perfume using her precious Silverstar, but Rowan's plans were very different.

DESERT ROMANCE
Irene Ord

Sally agrees to take her sister Pam's place as La Chartreuse the dancer, but she finds out there is more to it than dyeing her hair red and looking like her sister.

HEART OF ICE
Marie Sidney

How was January to know that not only would the warmth of the Swiss people thaw out her frozen heart, but that she too would play her part in helping someone to live again?

LUCKY IN LOVE
Margaret Wood

Companion-secretary to wealthy gambler Laura Duxford, who lived in Monaco, seemed to Melanie a fabulous job. Especially as Melanie had already lost her heart to Laura's son, Julian.

NURSE TO PRINCESS JASMINE
Lilian Woodward

Nick's surgeon brother, Tom, performs an operation on an Arabian princess, and she invites Tom, Nick and his fiancé to Omander, where a web of deceit and intrigue closes about them.

THE WAYWARD HEART
Eileen Barry

Disaster-prone Katherine's nickname was "Kate Calamity", but her boss went too far with an outrageous proposal, which because of her latest disaster, she could not refuse.

FOUR WEEKS IN WINTER
Jane Donnelly

Tessa wasn't looking forward to meeting Paul Mellor again — she had made a fool of herself over him once before. But was Orme Jared's solution to her problem likely to be the right one?

SURGERY BY THE SEA
Sheila Douglas

Medical student Meg hadn't really wanted to go and work with a G.P. on the Welsh coast although the job had its compensations. But Owen Roberts was certainly not one of them!

HEAVEN IS HIGH
Anne Hampson

The new heir to the Manor of Marbeck had been found. But it was rather unfortunate that when he arrived unexpectedly he found an uninvited guest, complete with stetson and high boots.

LOVE WILL COME
Sarah Devon

June Baker's boss was not really her idea of her ideal man, but when she went from third typist to boss's secretary overnight she began to change her mind.

ESCAPE TO ROMANCE
Kay Winchester

Oliver and Jean first met on Swale Island. They were both trying to begin their lives afresh, but neither had bargained for complications from the past.

CASTLE IN THE SUN
Cora Mayne

Emma's invalid sister, Kym, needed a warm climate, and Emma jumped at the chance of a job on a Mediterranean island. But Emma soon finds that intrigues and hazards lurk on the sunlit isle.

BEWARE OF LOVE
Kay Winchester

Carol Brampton resumes her nursing career when her family is killed in a car accident. With Dr. Patrick Farrell she begins to pick up the pieces of her life, but is bitterly hurt when insinuations are made about her to Patrick.

DARLING REBEL
Sarah Devon

When Jason Farradale's secretary met with an accident, her glamorous stand-in was quite unable to deal with one problem in particular.

THE PRICE OF PARADISE
Jane Arbor

It was a shock to Fern to meet her estranged husband on an island in the middle of the Indian Ocean, but to discover that her father had engineered it puzzled Fern. What did he hope to achieve?

DOCTOR IN PLASTER
Lisa Cooper

When Dr. Scott Sutcliffe is injured, Nurse Caroline Hurst has to cope with a very demanding private case. But when she realises her exasperating patient has stolen her heart, how can Caroline possibly stay?

A TOUCH OF HONEY
Lucy Gillen

Before she took the job as secretary to author Robert Dean, Cadie had heard how charming he was, but that wasn't her first impression at all.

ROMANTIC LEGACY
Cora Mayne

As kennelmaid to the Armstrongs, Ann Brown, had no idea that she would become the central figure in a web of mystery and intrigue.

THE RELENTLESS TIDE
Jill Murray

Steve Palmer shared Nurse Marie Blane's love of the sea and small boats. Marie's other passion was her step-brother. But when danger threatened who should she turn to — her step-brother or the man who stirred emotions in her heart?

ROMANCE IN NORWAY
Cora Mayne

Nancy Crawford hopes that her visit to Norway will help her to start life again. She certainly finds many surprises there, including unexpected happiness.

UNLOCK MY HEART
Honor Vincent

When Ruth Linton, a young widow wi   hildren, inherits a house in   country, it seems to be the answer to her dreams. But Ruth's problems were only just beginning . . .

SWEET PROMISE
Janet Dailey

Erica had met Rafael in Mexico, where their relationship had been brief but dramatic. Now, over a year later in Texas, she had met him again — and he had the power to wreck her life.

SAFARI ENCOUNTER
Rosemary Carter

Jenny had to accept that she couldn't run her father's game park alone; so she let forceful Joshua Adams virtually ta   ver. But Joshua took over her he... as well!